An invisible force drew her head round and she found herself looking out of the airplane window.

He stood on the tarmac, his eyes obscured by a pair of aviator sunglasses. The fact that he was allowed such unprecedented access to the runway said a great deal for the influence he wielded. No other civilian would have been extended such a privilege. But this man wasn't just anyone. He was a Ferrara. A member of one of the oldest and most powerful families in Sicily.

Stubborn, arrogant, controlling—why had he come to meet her? Was he punishing her or himself?

Her kindly neighbor craned her neck to get a better look. "Who do you think he is? They don't have a royal family, do they? Must be someone important. I wonder who he's meeting?"

"Me." Laurel rose to her feet with all the enthusiasm of a condemned woman preparing to walk to the gallows. "His name is Cristiano Ferrara and he's my husband."

Sarah Morgan

ONCE A FERRARA WIFE...

Harlequin®

TORONTO NEW YORK LONDON
AMSTERDAM PARIS SYDNEY HAMBURG
STOCKHOLM ATHENS TOKYO MILAN MADRID
PRAGUE WARSAW BUDAPEST AUCKLAND

Recycling programs
for this product may
not exist in your area.

ISBN-13: 978-0-373-23813-2

ONCE A FERRARA WIFE...

First North American Publication 2012

Copyright © 2011 by Sarah Morgan

Printed in U.S.A.

ONCE A FERRARA WIFE...

CHAPTER ONE

'LADIES *and gentlemen welcome to Sicily. Please keep your seat belts fastened until the aircraft has come to a standstill.'*

Laurel kept her eyes fixed on the book in her lap. She wasn't ready to look out of the window. Not yet. Too many memories waited there—memories she'd spent two years trying to erase.

The toddler in the row behind her yelled a protest and squirmed, smacking both his legs into the back of her seat with a force that jolted her forwards, but Laurel was aware of nothing except the hot ball of stress that burned at the base of her ribs. Normally reading soothed her but her eyes were recognising letters that her brain wouldn't compute. Even as part of her was wishing she'd packed a different book, another part of her knew it wouldn't have made a difference.

'You can let go of the seat now. We've landed.' The woman seated next to her touched her hand gently. 'My sister is a nervous flyer too.'

Laurel heard the quiet voice from somewhere in the distance and slowly turned her head. 'Nervous flyer?'

'It's nothing to be ashamed of. My sister once had a panic attack en route to Chicago. They had to sedate her. You've been gripping that seat since we took off from Heathrow. I said to my Bill, "That girl doesn't even know we're sitting next to her. And she hasn't once turned the page of that book." But we've landed now. It's over.'

Absorbing the startling truth that she hadn't turned the page once during the flight, Laurel stared at the woman blankly. Kind brown eyes looked back at her. The woman's expression was concerned and motherly.

Motherly?

Laurel was surprised she was even capable of recognising that expression, given that she'd never seen it before, especially not directed at her. She had no memory of being left wrapped in supermarket bags in a cold city park by a mother who didn't want her, but the memories of the years that followed were embedded in her brain like shrapnel.

She had no idea why she would suddenly feel tempted to confess to a stranger that her fear had nothing to do with flying and everything to do with landing—in Sicily.

The other woman filled the silence. 'We're safely down now. You can stop worrying.' She leaned over

Laurel and craned her neck to see out of the window. 'Just look at that blue sky and that view. It's my first time in Sicily. And you?'

Small talk. Conversation that skimmed the surface but never dipped into the murky ocean of feelings beneath.

This, Laurel could do. 'It's not my first time.' Because the woman's kindness deserved some reward, she added a smile to the words. 'I came here on business a few years ago.' Mistake number one, she thought.

The woman eyed Laurel's skinny jeans. 'And this time?'

Laurel's lips moved, the answers flowing automatically even though her brain was engaged elsewhere. 'I'm here for my best friend's wedding.'

'A real Sicilian wedding? Oh, that's so romantic. I saw that scene in *The Godfather*, all that dancing and family and friends—fabulous. And the Italians are so good with children, of course.' The woman threw a disapproving look at the passenger behind them who had read her book throughout the flight and ignored her fractious toddler. 'Family is everything to them.'

Laurel stuffed the book in her bag and undid her seat belt, suddenly desperate to escape from the conversation. 'You've been so kind. Sorry I've been such boring company on this flight. If you'll excuse me, I have to go.'

'Oh, no, dear, you can't leave your seat yet. Didn't you hear the announcement? There's someone important on the plane. Some VIP or other. Apparently they have to leave before the rest of us.' Peering past Laurel out of the window, the woman gave an excited gasp. 'Oh, just look at that. *Three* cars with blacked out windows have just pulled up. And those men look like bodyguards. And—oh, my, you *have* to look, dear, it's like something out of a movie. I swear they have guns. And the most gorgeous man you've ever seen has just stepped onto the tarmac. He's got to be at least six foot three and spectacular to look at!'

Man?

No, she wasn't expecting a man. She wasn't expecting anyone. To avoid an unwanted reception committee, she'd told no one which flight she would be on.

Her chest felt ominously tight and suddenly she wished she'd kept her asthma inhaler with her instead of putting it in her bag in the overhead locker.

An invisible force drew her head round and she found herself looking out of the window.

He stood on the tarmac, his eyes obscured by a pair of aviator sunglasses, his attention apparently fixed on the commercial aircraft that had just taxied to a halt. The fact that he was allowed such unprecedented access to the runway said a great deal for the influence he wielded. No other civilian would have been extended such a privilege, but this man wasn't just anyone. He was a Ferrara. A member of one of the oldest and most powerful families in Sicily.

Typical, Laurel thought. *When you want him, he's nowhere to be seen. And when you don't...*

Her kindly neighbour craned her neck to get a better look. 'Who do you think he is? They don't have a royal family, do they? Must be someone important if he can skip Customs and just drive onto the runway. And what sort of man needs all that security? I wonder who he's meeting?'

'Me.' Laurel rose to her feet with all the enthusiasm of a condemned man preparing to walk to the gallows. 'His name is Cristiano Domenico Ferrara and he's my husband.' Mistake number two, she thought numbly. But not for much longer. She was about to become an ex-wife. A wedding and a divorce in the same trip. Killing two birds with one stone.

She wondered about that saying. What was good about killing two birds?

'I hope you have a really nice holiday in Sicily. Make sure you try the *granita*. It's the best.' Ignoring the worried look of her kindly neighbour, Laurel removed her bag from the overhead locker and walked down the aisle to the front of the plane, grateful that she'd worn heels. There was something about high heels that gave you confidence in a tight situation and she was definitely in a tight situation. Passengers whispered and stared but Laurel was barely aware of them. She was too busy wondering how she could get through the next few days. It would be the biggest test of her life and she had a feeling it was going to take more than a pair of killer heels to see her safely through it.

Stubborn, arrogant, controlling—why had he come to meet her? Was he punishing her or himself?

The pilot hovered at the top of the metal steps. 'Signora Ferrara, we had no idea we had the pleasure of your company on board—' His forehead was shiny with sweat and he cast a nervous glance towards the formidable welcoming committee assembled on the tarmac. 'You should have made yourself known.'

'I didn't want to be known.'

His fawning attention was uncomfortable to witness. 'I hope you enjoyed your flight with us today.'

The journey couldn't have been more painful if she'd been tied to a cart and dragged back to Sicily.

How stupid of her to have thought she could just arrive in her own time and that no one would notice. Cristiano had probably had the airports monitored. Or maybe he had access to the passenger lists.

When they'd been together, the extent of his influence had left her open-mouthed with disbelief. In her job she was used to dealing with celebrities and the super-rich but the Ferrara world was nothing short of extraordinary.

For a short time she'd lived that life with him. That glittering, gilded life of immense wealth and privilege. It had been like tumbling onto a bed of goose down after a life spent sleeping on concrete.

Seeing him standing at the bottom of the aircraft steps, Laurel almost lost her footing. She hadn't seen him since that day. That awful day, the memory of which could still make her run to the bathroom and heave up her guts.

When Daniela had insisted that she stick to her promise and be her maid of honour Laurel should have pointed out the impact of that request on everyone involved. She'd thought there was no limit to what she'd do for friendship, but now she realised she'd been wrong about that. Unfortunately that clarity of thinking came too late.

Reaching into her bag, Laurel pulled out her sunglasses and put them on. If he was playing that game, then so was she.

With the pilot standing nervously behind her and all the passengers absorbed in the unfolding drama, she lifted her chin and stepped through the open door.

The sudden punch of heat was a shock after the chilly fog of London. The sun blazed down on her, spotlighting every reluctant step. Her heels clunked on the metal and the only thing preventing her from falling was her death grip on the rail. It was like descending into hell and he waited on the tarmac like the devil himself—tall, intimidating and unnaturally still, flanked by dark-suited security men who waited at a deferential distance for his command.

It was so different from the first time she'd arrived here, full of excitement and anticipation. She'd fallen in love with the island and the people.

And one man in particular.

This man.

She couldn't see his eyes, but she didn't need to see them to know what he was thinking. She could feel the tension—knew that he was being sucked back into the past just as she was.

'Cristiano.' At the last moment she remembered to inject casual indifference into her tone. 'You didn't have to break off from closing another mega-deal to come and meet me. I wasn't exactly expecting you to hang out the welcome flags.'

That hard, sensuous mouth flickered at the corners. 'How could I not meet my dear, sweet wife from the airport?'

After two barren years it was a shock to be face to face with him. But the bigger shock was the fierce hunger that burned in the empty pit of her stomach, the deep craven wanting she'd believed had died alongside their marriage.

Despair hit her because feeling like this felt like a betrayal of her beliefs.

She didn't *want* to feel like this.

Cristiano Ferrara was a cold, hard, unfeeling bastard who no longer deserved a place in her life.

No, not cold. Automatically she corrected herself. Not that. In fact it might have been easier had he been cold. To someone as emotionally cautious as Laurel, Cristiano with his volatile, expressive Sicilian temperament had been dangerously fascinating. She'd been seduced by his charisma, his blatant masculinity and by his refusal to let her hide from him. He'd dragged an honesty from her she'd never given to anyone else.

Now, she was grateful for the extra layer of protection provided by the sunglasses. She'd never been good at revealing her thoughts to anyone. She'd always protected herself. To trust him had taken all her courage, which had made his careless betrayal all the more shocking.

She didn't see him move but he must have gestured because one of the cars drew up next to her and a door opened.

'Get in the car, Laurel.' His icy tone wrapped itself around her body and acted like brakes. She couldn't move.

Laurel stared into the interior at the luxurious evidence of the Ferrara success story.

She was supposed to climb inside without question. To follow his wishes without question because that was what everyone else did. In the world he inhabited—a world outside the limits of most people's imagination—he was all powerful. He decided what happened and when.

Mistake number three had been coming back, she thought. Her anger, held tightly inside for two years, gnawed at her insides like acid.

She didn't want to slide into the car with him.

She didn't want to share that small, enclosed space with this man.

'I feel sick after the plane journey. I'm going to walk around Palermo for a while before I go to the hotel.' She'd booked somewhere small that would never appear on the Ferrara radar. Somewhere she could recover from the emotional demands of this wedding.

The breath hissed through his teeth. 'Get in the car or so help me I will put you there myself. Embarrass me in public again and you *will* regret it.'

Again. Because of course she had done exactly that. She'd taken his masculine pride and smashed it into pieces and he'd never forgiven her.

Which suited her fine because she'd never forgiven him, either.

Never forgiven him for abandoning her when she'd needed him most.

She couldn't forgive or forget, but that didn't matter because she had no desire to rekindle their relationship. She didn't want to fix what they'd broken.

This weekend wasn't about them, it was about his sister.

Her best friend.

Keeping that fact at the front of her mind, Laurel bent her head and slid into the car, grateful for the blacked out windows that shielded her from the goggling passengers who sat with their noses pressed to the windows of the aeroplane watching the drama unfold.

Cristiano joined her in the car and the door was closed on them. The doors locked with a solid clunk, a reminder that a member of the super-rich Ferrara family was always a target.

He leaned forward and spoke in Italian to the driver, the lilting expressive language sliding over Laurel with the softness of silk. He was an international businessman and he favoured Italian over the more guttural Sicilian dialect spoken by the locals although he could switch easily enough when it suited him. The fact that she loved hearing him speak to her in Italian had been one of their many private jokes.

The car moved forward, their departure allowing the rest of the passengers to finally disembark.

Laurel envied them their freedom. 'How did you know I would be on that flight?'

'Is that a serious question?'

No. If there was anything that the Ferrara family didn't know then it was because it didn't interest them. The scope and reach of their power was breathtaking, especially for someone like her who had come from nowhere. No one had cared who she was or where she was going.

'I didn't expect you to meet me. I was going to text Dani, or get a taxi or something.'

'Why?' His strong, muscular leg was dangerously close to hers, thrusting into her personal space. 'You wanted to find out if I'd pay the ransom if you were kidnapped?' Power throbbed from him and suddenly she realised why she'd been swept along by everything. She could barely think in his presence. Even now, his sexuality made her catch her breath.

She slid across the seat slightly, trying to widen the distance. 'The divorce will be final soon. You probably would have paid them to take me off your hands. Your stroppy, disobedient ex-wife.'

The tension in the car tightened to snapping point. 'Until the ink is dry on those papers, you're still a Ferrara. Act like one.'

Laurel leaned her head back against the seat.

Laurel Ferrara. A legal reminder that she'd made a bad decision. The name sounded better than the reality.

The large powerful Ferrara family was bound together by blood and centuries of history. Their name was synonymous with success, duty and tradition. Even his sister Daniela, for all her English university education and rebel ways, was settling down and marrying a Sicilian from a good family. Her future was mapped out. Secure. Within a year she'd have a baby. Then another. That was what the Ferraras did. They bred more Ferraras to continue the dynasty.

Laurel's throat burned and she stared straight ahead of her, grateful for the sunglasses that hid her eyes.

There were so many things she didn't allow herself to think about. So many places she didn't allow her mind to visit.

It had been more than two years since she'd seen him and she'd disciplined herself not to look at his photograph or surf the Internet for images, knowing that the only way to survive was to try and wipe him from her brain. But that wasn't easily done with this man.

Once seen, never forgotten. Cristiano was so insanely good-looking that wherever he went, women stared. And it had driven her mad even though he'd done nothing to attract that attention except be himself.

Her need proved stronger than her willpower and she glanced sideways.

Even dressed casually in black jeans and an open-necked polo shirt he looked spectacular and her body responded instantly to the raw male power that was so much a part of who he was. He would no more have apologised for his masculinity than would his caveman ancestors. His masculinity was his pride. And she'd dealt that pride a lethal blow.

'Why didn't Dani come with you to meet me?'

'My sister believes in happy endings.'

What was that supposed to mean? That Daniela thought by allowing them to be alone together they'd fall into each other's arms and heal a rift wider than the Grand Canyon?

Laurel thought about all Dani's clumsy match-making attempts at college. 'She always did believe in fairy tales.' A long forgotten memory appeared through the haze of misery. A child's room, complete with a canopy bed and pretty fairy lights. Shelves of books, all portraying life as a joyful adventure. A fantasy room. Annoyed with herself for thinking of that now, she shook her head slightly, dislodging the image from her mind. 'Dani is an incurable romantic. I guess that's why she's getting married despite—' She broke off but he finished her sentence.

'—despite witnessing the wreckage of our marital car crash? Given your relaxed attitude to marriage vows, I'm staggered that you agreed to act as maid of honour. A decision bordering on the hypocritical, don't you think?'

He shifted the blame onto her, absolving himself of all responsibility, and Laurel didn't bother arguing because she didn't want to change the outcome. If he hated her, fine. If anything, his animosity helped because it poisoned those dangerous feelings that still lurked deep inside.

As for being Dani's maid of honour—

Laurel had thought of a million reasons to say no but none of them had come out of her mouth when talking to her friend. Mistake number four, she thought. How had she made so many? 'I'm a loyal friend.'

'Loyal?' Slowly and deliberately, he removed his sunglasses and looked at her, those thickly lashed dark eyes revealing the depth of his own struggle. 'You dare speak of loyalty? Perhaps this is a language thing because we definitely don't have the same definition of that word.' Unlike her, he didn't hide his emotions. Instead he spilled them over her and the more honest he was, the more she withdrew. She was struggling to handle her own feelings. She certainly couldn't handle his.

Drowning under the full force of his contempt, she pressed herself back against the seat, trying to calm her breathing. She could have hurled her own accusations but that would have taken them back to the past and all she wanted to do was move forwards. Her limbs were trembling and the tips of her fingers were suddenly ice-cold.

Knowing how important it was to control her stress levels, she forced herself to breathe slowly. 'If you're going to go for one of your volatile Sicilian Mount Etna-like explosions, at least wait until we're behind closed doors. It's just a wedding. We can get through this without killing each other.'

'*Just* a wedding? So weddings are no big deal, is that right, Laurel?'

'Let's not do this, Cristiano.' He was incapable of seeing that he might have been wrong. Incapable of apologising. She knew that the absence of the word *sorry* from his vocabulary had nothing to do with his linguistic ability and everything to do with his ego.

'Why? Because emotion frightens you? Admit it. You're terrified of what you feel when you're with me. You've always been terrified.'

'Oh, please—'

'It burns you up, doesn't it?' His voice was silky-smooth and dangerous. 'It frightens you so badly you have to push it away. That's why you left.'

'You think I left because I was afraid of how much I loved you?' Outrage lit the fires of her own response. 'You are so unbelievably arrogant you need a whole island just to house your ego. Are you sure Sicily is big enough? Maybe you should buy Sardinia, too!'

'I'm working on it.' His laconic reply was delivered without a hint of irony. 'If you're so indifferent, then why haven't you been back?'

'There was nothing to come back for.' And every reason to stay away. Laurel stared straight forward, trying to control her thoughts, feeling his gaze on her.

'You look good. Relieving all that stress with exercise?'

'Fitness is my job. It's how I earn my living. And I'm back because of your sister, not because of u—' the word jammed itself on all the barriers she'd erected between them '—you or me.'

'You can't even say it, can you? *Us, tesoro*. The word you struggle with is *us*. But the concept of being part of an *us* has always been your biggest challenge.' Cristiano lounged back in his seat, relaxed and maddeningly sure of himself. 'Probably best not to use the word *loyal* again in reference to yourself, either. That one really presses my buttons. I'm sure you understand.'

Laurel felt like a matador trapped with a very angry bull with nothing for protection but her own anger. And that anger burned slow and dangerous because he was behaving as if he'd played no part in the demise of their relationship.

He just couldn't see it, she thought numbly. He just didn't see what he'd done wrong.

And that made it a thousand times worse.

One *sorry* might have healed it, but to say sorry Cristiano would first have had to admit fault.

Reminding herself of her determination not to discuss the past, she changed the subject. 'How is Dani?'

'Looking forward to officially becoming an *us*. Unlike you, she has no fear of intimacy.'

She remembered thinking once that their relationship was too perfect and time had proved her right. Perfection had proved as fragile as spun sugar.

'If you are going to carry on taking bites out of me perhaps I'd better just get on the next flight home.'

'And make things easy for you? I don't think so. You are our guest of honour, after all.'

His tone made her flinch more than the words themselves, because it was tinged with a bitterness and regret that stung her wounds like the juice of the Sicilian lemon.

Occasionally, when the pain grew almost too much to bear, she asked herself if her life would have been better if she'd never met him. She'd always known that life was hard, which was why meeting Cristiano Ferrara had been like falling straight into a starring role in her own fairy tale. What she hadn't known was how much harder life would be once she'd given him up.

'It's obvious that coming here wasn't one of my better ideas.'

'If this was anything other than Dani's wedding you wouldn't be allowed to set foot on the island.'

She didn't state the obvious. That if this was anything other than his sister's wedding, she wouldn't have been here.

The divorce could have been handled at a distance. And Laurel preferred distance in everything.

They'd been driving for fifteen minutes, through chaotic Palermo with its jumble of streets littered with Gothic and baroque churches and ancient palaces. Somewhere in the centre was the Palazzo Ferrara, Cristiano's city residence, now occasionally used as an exclusive venue for weddings and concerts, its wonderful mosaics and baroque ceiling frescos drawing academics and tourists from around the world. It was one of many homes that Cristiano owned around the island but he rarely used it as a base.

Laurel had fallen in love with it and tried not to think about the tiny private chapel that had been the setting for their wedding.

She knew that, despite his aristocratic lineage and his encyclopaedic knowledge of Sicilian art and architecture, he preferred living in modern surroundings with state-of-the-art technology at his fingertips. Cristiano without Internet access would be like Michelangelo without a paintbrush.

Glancing out of the window, she saw that they'd emerged from the choked Palermo traffic and were speeding along the coast road that led to the Ferrara Spa Resort, the ultimate destination for the discerning traveller and one of the top hotels in the world.

It was a hideaway for the glitterati, for that stratosphere of international society that craved privacy and seclusion. Here it was guaranteed, both by the legendary Ferrara security but also by the geography of the coastline. The Ferrara brothers had built the exclusive hotel on a spit of land surrounded on three sides by private beach and spread across lush gardens, dotted with luxury villas. It was a Mediterranean paradise, each individual villa offering the ultimate in pampered seclusion.

The pain of being back here was intensified by the memories that were carved in every glimpse of the place because it had been here, in the exclusive villa on a rocky promontory at the far end of the private beach, that they'd spent the first nights of their honeymoon. It was the villa that Cristiano had built for his own use. The ultimate bachelor pad.

Laurel stiffened. Surely they hadn't booked her a room in the hotel? 'I booked a hotel outside the resort.'

'I know exactly where you were staying. My staff cancelled the booking. You'll stay where I put you and be grateful for Sicilian hospitality that makes it impossible for us to turn away a guest.'

Her stomach churned. 'My plan was to stay elsewhere and arrive just for the wedding.'

'Daniela wants you to be part of all of it. Tonight is a gathering of local people. Black tie. Drinks and dancing. As her maid of honour, you are expected to join in.'

Drinks and dancing?

Laurel felt cold and wished his driver would turn off the air conditioning. 'Obviously I don't expect to be part of the pre-wedding celebrations. I have my laptop so I can just get on with some work. I'm buried under a mountain of it at the moment.'

'I don't care. You'll be there and you'll smile. Our separation is amicable and civilized, remember?'

Civilized?

There was nothing civilized about the emotions spinning inside her and nothing civilized about the dangerous glint in his eyes. Their relationship had never been civilized, she thought numbly. The passion they'd shared had been scorching, crazy and out of control. Unfortunately all that heat had burned through her ability to think clearly.

Laurel tried to breathe normally, but the prospect of facing his family was impossibly daunting. They all hated her, of course. And part of her understood that. From their point of view she was the English girl who'd given up on the marriage and that was unforgivable in the circles in which he moved. In Sicily marriages endured. Affairs, if they happened, were overlooked.

She had no idea what the rule book said for handling what had happened to them. No idea what the rules were for coping with the shocking loss of a pregnancy and a monumentally selfish husband.

The only thing that comforted her in the whole disastrous episode had been that Dani, generous extrovert Dani, had refused to judge her. And the downside of that acceptance was that she was here now, putting herself through hell for the only true friend she'd ever had.

'I'll do whatever people want me to do.' It was a performance, she thought. If she had to smile, she'd smile. If she were expected to dance, she'd dance. The outside didn't have to reflect the inside. She'd learned that as a child. She'd learned to bury her feelings deep, so deep that few ever saw them.

Her confidence that she could cope with the situation lasted until they drove through the entrance gates and she realised the driver was taking the private road towards the Aphrodite Villa. The jewel in the crown. Cristiano's beachside bolt-hole, his personal retreat from the demands placed on him by his thriving business empire.

When they'd built the Resort they'd used part of the land to relocate their corporate headquarters and Laurel had never ceased to drool over his office, which exploited the stunning coastal position. Cristiano had qualified as a structural engineer and his talents in that area were visible in the innovative design features incorporated into his headquarters.

As would be expected, the walls of his office were glass. What was unexpected was the floor, also glass and stretching out over the water so that a visitor to his office could find himself distracted by shoals of colourful Mediterranean fish darting beneath their feet.

It was typical of Cristiano to merge the aesthetic with the functional and there were similar touches throughout his hotels.

'I don't see why an office has to be a boring box in the centre of a smog-choked city,' he'd said when she'd gasped at her first sight of his office. 'I like the sea. This way, if I'm stuck behind my desk, I can still enjoy it.'

It was that same breadth of vision that had made the company so successful. That, and his sophistication and appreciation for luxury. Her first glimpse of the Aphrodite Villa had made her jaw drop, but going there now drew a very different response from her.

The shock of it tore a hole in her composure. 'Why are we going this way? I'm not staying here.' It was too reminiscent of their wedding night, when she'd been so happy and full of optimism for the future.

'Why would you care where you sleep?' His tone was hard and unsympathetic. 'If what we shared was "just a wedding," then presumably this was "just a honeymoon", in which case the place holds no sentimental value. It's just a bed.'

Laurel struggled to bring her breathing back to normal. She carried an asthma inhaler in her bag but there was no way she was going to use it in front of him unless she was half dead.

And now she was trapped. To admit how the place made her feel would be to reveal something she had no intention of ever revealing.

Not to admit it meant staying here.

'It's your premium property.' Occasionally, she knew, he had been persuaded to loan it to honeymooning rock stars and actors. 'Why waste it on me?'

'It's the only vacant bed in the place. Sleep in it and be grateful.' His tone was so chilly and matter-of-fact that for a moment she truly believed that the villa held no significance for him whatsoever. For a man who owned five homes and spent his working life travelling the world, this was just another few hundred square metres of luxurious accommodation.

Or was it?

Was he doing this to punish her?

'Well, at least it has a good internet connection.' She kept her eyes ahead, refusing to let him access her secrets. She tried not to remember that gazing into his eyes had once been her favourite pastime. On more than one occasion she'd woken him just so that she could experience that incredible connection that happened whenever they looked at each other. With him, she'd discovered intimacy. But intimacy meant openness and openness meant vulnerability, as she'd learned to her cost.

He'd demanded that she trust him and gradually she'd yielded to that because he would accept nothing less. And then he had let her down so badly she doubted the bruises would ever heal.

'You're being treated as an honoured guest. We both know it's more than you deserve. Let's go.' Without giving her the chance to argue further, he opened the door and sprang from the car with that same driven sense of purpose that characterised everything he did.

All he could focus on was the fact that she'd left him, Laurel thought numbly. It was all about his pride. Not about their relationship. He saw himself as the injured party.

She had no choice but to follow him up the pathway that led to the villa. Inside, she knew, there would be air conditioning so there would be some relief from the blistering Sicilian sun. Unless it was the chemistry between them that burned hotter than the fires of hell.

Cristiano flung open the door and she heard the sound of the car reversing as his driver retreated back to the main hotel complex.

Laurel stepped across the threshold, trying not to remember their wedding night when he'd carried her through the door, both of them frantic in their indecent desperation for each other. 'Why isn't he waiting for you?'

He dropped her case onto the tiled floor. 'Why do you think? Because I'm staying here too.'

The words floated right past her because they made no sense.

'Please tell me that's a joke—' Her voice sounded strange, robotic. 'There's only one bedroom.' One enormous bedroom overlooking the pool and the beach. The bedroom where they'd spent long sultry nights together.

Cristiano gave a bitter smile. 'Blame Dani again. Her wedding. Her room allocation.'

'I'm not sharing a bed with you!' The words flew out before she could stop them and he turned with an angry snarl that was animal-like in its ferocity.

'You think you need to say that to me? Do you think I would have you back in my bed after what you did? *Do you?*'

Her heart was hammering and she took an instinctive step backwards even though she knew he'd never hurt her. Not physically. 'I can't stay here with you.' The emotions she'd kept locked down during the horrendous car journey were bubbling up like milk on the boil, refusing to be contained. 'It's too—'

'It's too what?' Something about the way he was looking at her made her heart beat faster. He'd always been frighteningly good at reading her mind and this time it was imperative that he didn't.

She didn't want to open up. It was way too late for that.

Grateful for years of practice at hiding what she felt, Laurel hauled her emotions back inside her. 'It's awkward,' she said coldly. 'For both of us.'

He stared at her for another few seconds and then his mouth hardened. 'I think "awkward" is the least of our problems, don't you? Don't worry. I'll sleep on the couch. And if you're worried that I won't be able to keep my hands off you, then don't be. You had your chance.' Insultingly indifferent, he strolled away from her but even that didn't give her breathing space because there were traces of him everywhere.

A tailored jacket slung carelessly over the back of a chair. The glass of fresh Sicilian lemonade, half drunk because he'd been disturbed and too busy to finish. His laptop, the battery light glowing because he worked such long hours he never bothered to shut down. All those things were so familiar, so much a part of him, and for a moment she stood still, unable to breathe, swamped by a longing to turn the clock back.

But turn it back to when?

How could there have ever been a different outcome?

Their love had been doomed from the beginning.
Together they'd managed to make Romeo and
Juliet look like a match made in heaven.

CHAPTER TWO

CRISTIANO downed the glass of whisky in one, trying to blunt the savage bite of his emotions as he waited on the terrace of the villa for Laurel to make an appearance.

He'd promised himself that he would be icily calm and detached. That resolution had lasted until she'd stepped off the plane. His plan to make no reference to their situation had exploded under the intense pressure of the reunion. The conflicting emotions had been like a storm inside him, made all the more fierce by her own lack of response. Laurel had turned hiding her emotions into an art form.

Wishing he had time to go for a run and burn off some of the adrenalin scalding his veins, Cristiano lifted a hand and slid a finger into the collar of his white dress shirt. Deprived of one stress reliever, he reached for another and topped up his glass with a hand that wasn't quite steady.

She still blamed him. That much was obvious but, even now, she wouldn't talk about it.

Immediately after the event he'd tried, but she'd appeared to be in shock, her reaction to the miscarriage far more extreme than he would have anticipated.

His own sadness at the loss of their baby had been tempered with a sense of realism. Miscarriages happened. His own mother had lost two babies. His aunt, one. It was Laurel's first pregnancy. He'd been philosophical.

She'd been inconsolable.

And stubborn.

Apart from that one message on his voicemail, *the one telling him not to bother to cut short his meeting because she'd lost the baby,* she'd refused to talk about what had happened.

Sweat prickled the back of his neck and he wished for the millionth time he hadn't switched off his phone before going into that meeting.

If he'd answered the call, would they be in a different place now?

Contemplating the celebration that lay ahead made him want to empty the bottle of whisky. He was in desperate need of an anaesthetic to dull his senses and relieve the pain.

Maybe it was because his own marriage was such a total disaster that he hated weddings so much.

Part of him wished his sister had just eloped quietly, but that had never been on the cards. She was marrying a Sicilian man in true Sicilian style and he, as her older brother and the head of the family, was expected to play a major part in the celebrations. The family honour was at stake. The image of the Ferrara dynasty. He was expected to celebrate.

'I'm ready.' Her voice came from behind him and this time he made sure that he had himself fully under control before he turned.

Even prepared, the connection was immediate and powerful.

It was like being trapped in an electrical storm. The air around him crackled and buzzed with a tension that hadn't been there before she'd stepped over the threshold.

Ready? He almost laughed. Neither of them would ever be ready for what they were about to face. Their estrangement had attracted almost as much attention as their wedding. There would be no cameras tonight, but that didn't mean the guests wouldn't be interested. With that macabre fascination that drew people to stare at the wreckage of car accidents, everyone was waiting to see how he was going to treat his scandalous estranged wife.

Looking at her, he felt the attraction punch through his gut. Her body was slim and supremely fit and wrapped in a dress of fine blue silk. On most women the dress would have been monumentally unforgiving. Laurel had nothing that needed forgiving. Her body was her brand and she dressed to showcase it and drive her business. It wouldn't have surprised him to see her web address stamped on her hemline. Ferrara Fitness. He'd been the one who had spotted her potential and persuaded her to expand—to broaden what she offered from the personal to the corporate.

She wasn't beautiful in a classical sense, but her guts and drive had proved a greater aphrodisiac than sleek blonde hair or a perfect D cup. Only he knew that her restrained appearance and tiger-like personality hid monumental insecurities.

From the outside no one would ever have guessed that on the inside she was such a mess, he mused, but he'd never met anyone more screwed up than Laurel. It had taken months for her to open up to him even a little and, when she had, the cold reality of her childhood had shocked him. It was a story of care homes and neglect, and just a brief glimpse into what her life had been was enough for him to begin to understand why she was so different from most of the women he met.

Had it been arrogance, he wondered, that had made him so sure that he could break down those defensive barriers? He'd demanded trust from someone who had never had reason to give it and, in the end, it had backfired badly.

Any residual guilt he might have felt about his own behaviour at that time had long been erased by his anger that she hadn't even given him a chance to fix his mistake. She'd ended their marriage with the finality of an executioner, refusing both rational conversation and the diamonds he'd bought her by way of apology.

Dark emotions swirled inside him and he studied her face for signs that she was regretting her decision. Her features were blank, but that didn't surprise him. She'd trained herself to reveal nothing. To rely on no one. Extracting anything from her had been a challenge.

Even now she chose to keep the conversation neutral. 'You changed the room overlooking the garden from a gym to a cinema.'

She would have noticed, of course, because that was her job. And Laurel was one hundred per cent committed to her job. Which was why they'd wanted her involved in the business. From the moment her success with one very overweight actress had been blazoned over the press, Laurel Hampton had become the personal trainer that everyone wanted. The fact that she'd agreed to advise the hotel had been a coup for both of them. He had her name on his brand and she had his. It had been a winning combination.

Hampton had become Ferrara.

And that was when the combination had exploded.

'I watch sport. I don't need a gym when I'm here.' Cristiano felt a flicker of exasperation. Their marriage was writhing in its death throes and they were discussing gym equipment?

Something glinted around her neck and he frowned at the thin gold chain. The fact that she was wearing jewellery he didn't recognise racked his tension levels up a few more notches and drove all thoughts from his brain. He hadn't given her the chain, so where the hell had it come from?

He pictured a pair of male hands fastening the necklace around her slender throat. Someone else touching her. Someone else persuading her to part with her secrets—

It was something that hadn't occurred to him before now.

Only when he heard the splintering sound of glass on ceramic tiles did he realise he'd dropped the glass he was holding.

Eyeing him as she would an escaped tiger, Laurel backed away. 'I'll get a brush—'

'Leave it.'

'But—'

'I said, leave it. The staff will sort it out. We need to go. I'm the host.'

'Everyone will be speculating.'

'They wouldn't dare. At least, not publicly.'

She gave a bitter laugh. 'Sorry. I forgot you even manage to control people's thoughts.'

Suddenly Cristiano wished he hadn't dropped the glass. God only knew he needed something to get him through the next few hours. The gold necklace glinted in the sunshine, taunting him. Following an impulse he didn't want to examine too closely, he grabbed her left hand and lifted it. She made a sound in her throat and tugged but he simply tightened his grip, shocked by the emotion that tore through him when he saw her bare finger.

'Where is your wedding ring?'

'I don't wear it. We're no longer married.'

'We're married until we're divorced and in Sicily that takes three years—' Teeth gritted, tone thickened, he held tightly to her hand as she twisted her fingers and tried to free herself.

'It's a bit late to be possessive. Marriage is about more than a ring, Cristiano, and more than a piece of paper.'

'*You* are telling *me* what constitutes marriage? You, who treated our marriage as something disposable?' Outrage and fury mingled in a lethal cocktail. 'Why remove your ring? Is there someone else?'

'This weekend isn't about us, it's about your sister.'

He'd wanted a denial.

He'd wanted her to laugh and say, *Of course there isn't anyone else—how could there be?*

He'd wanted her to admit that what they'd shared had been rare and special. Instead she was dismissing it. She'd consigned it to the dustbin of past mistakes.

Driven by an emotion he didn't understand, he grabbed her shoulders and yanked her against him. If he'd been more controlled he might have asked himself why he was trying to goad her, but he didn't feel controlled. The fact that she seemed indifferent simply intensified his urge to draw a response from her.

Caught off balance, she swayed against him. That brief whisper of contact was all it took. Thin blue silk proved an ineffectual barrier and the heat spread from him to her. He heard her breathing quicken and felt the powerful surge of desire as his body acknowledged her response. It confirmed what he already knew—that the chemistry between them was as powerful as ever. *Not indifferent*, he thought with grim satisfaction. It was the one emotion she couldn't mask. In a moment he'd be kissing her and he knew from bitter experience that once they kissed that was it. There was no turning back from it and it seemed that even after her betrayal that hadn't changed.

'There is no one else.' Her voice reflected all those painful emotions right back at him. 'One lousy relationship in a lifetime is enough.'

The words acted like a bucket of cold water over the flickering flames.

Cristiano released her as suddenly as he'd grabbed her. If he'd felt like laughing he would have laughed at himself. All his life women had thrown themselves at him. He'd taken it as a right that he could win any woman he wanted. And then he'd met Laurel and been slapped in the face with his own arrogance.

He stepped back from her, needing the distance. 'We're expected to attend this dinner. Let's get it over with.'

For once, the mask slipped. 'I'm going to call Dani and explain that I'm tired. She'll understand.'

It was true that her face was pale and her eyes huge but he knew that her reluctance to socialise had nothing to do with fatigue.

Cristiano wondered how far he could push her before she stopped guarding her every word. The ridiculous thing was, they had yet to talk about what had happened. She'd refused to have that conversation. 'Why would your conscience bother you now when it didn't bother you two years ago? Or is it just cowardice because you're embarrassed to meet my family? You came because of your loyalty to my sister so let's see that loyalty in action.' He'd never seen anyone so pale but before he could say anything she turned and walked quickly past him up the narrow path that snaked through the pretty gardens and led to the main part of the hotel. Apparently accepting her fate, she kept walking, her high heels tapping on the stones, her hair twisted into a severe knot that exposed her slender neck.

His gaze slid lower, to the dip of her waist and the curve of her bottom.

Squats, he thought savagely. She'd sculpted that bottom from squats and squat thrusts. So what?

His mood turbulent, Cristiano strode after her, resisting the temptation to flatten her against the nearest tree and demand to know what had been going through her crazy, mixed up mind when she'd smashed everything they'd created together. He wanted to *force* the issue she was avoiding out into the open. But most of all he wanted to rip that delicate gold chain from her throat and replace it with one of the jewels he'd given her when they'd been together. Something that announced to the world that she was *his*.

Unsettled by the depths to which his thoughts had sunk, it took him a moment to register that Laurel had stopped dead in the entrance to the terrace.

'Laurel.' Santo stood there. Santiago, his younger brother, hot-headed and overprotective, who felt responsible for the current mess because he was the one who had appointed Laurel as his personal trainer when he'd committed to run the New York City Marathon. Without that introduction, Cristiano never would have met her.

Santo glowered at her, his expression uncensored.

Laurel met that threatening stare without flinching. Despite his heightened emotions, Cristiano felt a flicker of reluctant admiration. Here she was, surrounded by people who felt nothing but animosity for her and she faced them head on. She barely reached his shoulder and yet it didn't occur to her to back down. Laurel was a fighter.

And that was part of the problem, he thought wearily. She was so used to defending herself that persuading her to lower her guard was virtually impossible.

Knowing that if they were to stand any chance of getting through the evening without an explosion he had to be the one to keep things calm, Cristiano stepped forward and took control. 'Is Daniela here?'

'She's waiting to make an entrance.' Santo's icy gaze was fixed on Laurel, who stared right back, almost willing him to come at her.

Eyeing the stubborn lift of her chin, Cristiano felt a flash of exasperation. 'You're neglecting our guests, Santo.' Deciding that a show of solidarity would calm the situation, he forced himself to take Laurel's hand and was shocked to find it ice-cold. Her fingers shook slightly in his. Surprised by that outward manifestation of emotion, he glanced at her face but she wasn't looking at him. Instead she tugged at her hand but he held her fast. Perhaps if he'd done that two years ago she wouldn't have flown, he thought grimly. Her crazy, disastrous childhood had left her with insecurities deeper than the ocean. On the surface she was a bright, competent businesswoman. Underneath she was emotional quicksand. He'd thought he could cope with that. He'd thought he was sane and well adjusted enough for both of them.

He'd been wrong.

As Santo turned away to greet some guests, Laurel turned to Cristiano with a fierce stare. 'You don't need to protect me.'

Cristiano released her. 'I wasn't protecting you. I was protecting my family. This is Dani's night and we don't need a scene.'

'I had no intention of creating a scene. You're the ones who can't hang onto your emotions. I'm perfectly in control.'

And that was the problem. It had always been the problem.

Cristiano bit back the comment he wanted to make. 'We're not going to do this, Laurel. Not here. Not now.'

'I don't want to do it at all.'

'Laurie?' Daniela's voice came from behind them and then there was a flash of vivid green and a soft swish of silk as she pushed past Santo and flung her arms around Laurel. 'You're here! I have so much to tell you. I need to sneak you away for just five minutes so that I can show you something.' Without giving Laurel the chance to respond, she took her hand and drew her away from Cristiano and towards the villa.

And Cristiano watched her go, wondering how

his sister had managed to penetrate that protective shell while he'd been locked out.

Having dispatched the latest arrivals to the terrace with a glass of champagne, Santo joined him, his face like a storm cloud.

'Why did you agree to this?'

'It was what Dani wanted.'

'But the last thing you need. Tell me that you're not, even for a moment, thinking of taking her back.'

Cristiano watched Laurel from the terrace, arm in arm with his sister. She moved with the grace of a dancer and the strength of an athlete, the subtle sway of her hips unconsciously sensual. Her knowledge of sports physiology was encyclopaedic and as for how she was in bed—

He clenched his jaw. 'I'm not thinking of taking her back.'

'No?' Santo's eyes followed a pretty blonde as she walked past and waved at him. 'Some men wouldn't blame you if you did. Laurel is undeniably hot.'

'If you don't want to give our sister away with a black eye,' Cristiano growled, 'don't describe my wife as "hot".'

'She isn't your wife. She's your soon-to-be ex-wife. The sooner the better.'

'I thought you liked Laurel?'

'That was before she left you.' Santo was still looking at the blonde. 'My advice? She isn't worth the effort. Let some other man have her.'

A red mist rose up from nowhere and the next minute Cristiano had smashed his fist into his brother's jaw and had him pinned against the wall.

It took Santo a moment to recover from the shock and then he hurled his weight against his brother and switched positions. This time it was Cristiano who found himself slammed against the wall. Hard stone pressed through the thin silk of his shirt and he felt the iron strength in his brother's hands holding him trapped. Trapped, along with all that anger.

'*Basta!* Stop, the pair of you.' It was Carlo, a life-long friend of Cristiano's who was also the family lawyer handling the divorce. He wrenched the two men apart and stood between them as Santo touched his fingers to his bruised jaw, his eyes on Cristiano.

Slowly, Carlo released his grip on Santo's shoulder. '*Calma*. Calm down. I haven't seen the two of you fight since you were sixteen. What is going on here?'

Santo's eyes were fixed on his brother. 'I suggested he should let another man have Laurel.'

Cristiano stepped forward again but Carlo's hand planted itself in the centre of his chest.

Surprisingly calm, Santo stepped back and adjusted his bow tie. 'Help yourself to champagne, Carlo. We're good.'

The lawyer glanced towards the terrace but mercifully no one seemed to have noticed the disturbance. 'Are you sure? A moment ago you were out of control.'

'I was never out of control—' Santo licked his split lip '—but I wanted an answer to a question and now I have it.' As Carlo reluctantly left them alone, Santo gave Cristiano a long, steady look. 'If this is love I'm glad I've managed to avoid it for so long because it looks like hell from where I'm standing.'

Cristiano felt the back of his neck tingle. 'It isn't love.'

'No?' Blotting blood from his mouth with the back of his hand, Santo lifted an eyebrow. 'If it's not, you might want to ask yourself why you knocked me in the dirt for the first time in almost two decades.'

'You suggested—' He couldn't even bring himself to say the words and Santo gave an unapologetic shrug.

'It was a test of how far you've come in the last two years. The answer is not far.' He grabbed two glasses of champagne from a waitress and handed one to his brother. 'Drink. You're going to need it. I thought you were in trouble before, but you're in bigger trouble than even I imagined.'

'Cristiano just punched Santo. Which is a nightmare actually because now he'll have a bruised jaw in my wedding photos.' Hitching up her dress so that she wouldn't crease it, Dani knelt on the window seat so that she could get a better look at the courtyard below. 'And now Santo's got him pinned against the wall. I haven't seen them fight since they were teenagers. My money's on Cristiano but it could be a close run thing.'

Imagining Cristiano still and lifeless, Laurel flew to the window in a panic. 'Is he hurt? Oh, God, someone should pull Santo off—'

'Cristiano is fine. He's still the stronger of the two.' Dani shot her a look. 'I thought you didn't care about him any more?'

'Just because I don't love him any more doesn't mean I want to see him hurt.' Laurel licked her lips. 'What do you think they're fighting about?'

'*You*, of course. What else?' Dani glanced enviously at Laurel's waist. 'You look good for someone in the middle of a relationship trauma. I'd do anything for your abs.'

'Anything except exercise,' Laurel said drily and Dani grinned.

'You know me so well. I lift my wine glass. Doesn't that count?'

Laurel turned her head to look out of the window again. 'I don't want them fighting over me.' The thought of Cristiano injured made her feel physically sick. Telling herself that was a perfectly normal reaction, she sank down onto the window seat next to Dani. 'Go down there and stop them.'

'No way. I might get blood on my dress. Do you like it? It's by that Italian designer that everyone

is wearing.' Dani smoothed the fabric. 'It's tradi-
tional to wear green the night before the wedding.
But you know that, of course, because you wore that
gorgeous green dress the night before you married
Cristiano.'

Laurel's chest felt ominously tight. The feeling
had grown gradually worse since that awful car
journey from the airport. Nothing she did could
calm it down.

Recognising the warning signs of an impending
asthma attack, she discreetly opened her bag and
checked that she had her inhaler. For her the trigger had always been stress and her stress levels had
been steadily rising since she'd arrived in Sicily. 'I
don't want to talk about my wedding.'

'You chose a better shade of green than me. In
the end I went for emerald but I'm wondering if for-
est would have been better. Because my hair is so
dark, I decided I needed the brightness of colour.'

'How can you even think about clothes when your
brothers are fighting?'

'I grew up watching my brothers fight so it's not
a big deal, although I must admit it's much more
fun now they're both more muscular. You only need
to worry when their shirts come off.' Dani craned
her neck to take another look. 'You should be flat-
tered. It's pretty cool having men fighting over you.
Romantic.'

'It isn't cool and there's nothing romantic about

two men who can't control their tempers.' Laurel wished she could just stay here. Hide away for the whole evening. 'I don't want them fighting.'

'Physically they're evenly matched, but a man defending the woman he loves is probably stronger, which is why Cristiano has the advantage. I *love* those shoes you're wearing. Did you get those in London?'

Laurel sprang from the window seat and walked the shoes to the far side of the room where she couldn't be tempted to look down into the courtyard. 'Cristiano doesn't love me. We barely tolerate each other.'

'Right. Which is why you're pacing and he's pounding Santo. You're both *so* indifferent to each other.' Exasperated, Dani dragged her gaze from Laurel's feet to her face. 'Do you know how many women have chased after Cristiano since he hit his teens?'

Laurel was horrified by how much that thought bothered her. 'Why is that relevant?'

'He picked *you*. That means a lot. I know he isn't always easy, but he *does* love you.'

'He picked me because I said no to him. Your brother isn't good with the word *no*. I was a challenge.'

'He picked you because he fell in love with you. And that is a huge thing for him.'

Amongst his family and colleagues, Cristiano

held a god-like status, Laurel acknowledged numbly. He walked on water. His word was law. 'We should be talking about *you*. Are you excited about tomorrow?'

'Of course I am! I'm as excited about my wedding as you were about yours.'

'That was completely different.'

'How?'

'You've been planning this wedding for over a year.'

'And you were married in a hurry in the family chapel because neither of you could wait any longer. I happen to think that's more romantic.'

The conversation was like treading on a pine cone in bare feet. It was prickly and uncomfortable. 'It was impulsive, not romantic.' Laurel rubbed her hands down her bare arms to warm them. 'If we'd spent a year planning it we wouldn't be in this mess now.'

'My brother has always been decisive. He doesn't take ages to think about something.'

'You mean he ploughs his way over people. He doesn't believe anyone else can have an opinion worth hearing.'

'No, I mean he knows what he wants.' Dani gave her a long look. 'Ouch. Things obviously became pretty rough between you. Do you want to talk about this?'

'Absolutely not.'

'Before he met you, he never mentioned marriage,' Dani said softly, clearly torn between her loyalty towards her friend and her brother. 'For a man like Cristiano that was the ultimate declaration of love.'

The ultimate declaration of love.

It was unfortunate he'd thought his responsibility ended there.

He'd put the ring on her finger. The ultimate gesture to go with the ultimate declaration. And that was his part of it done. All she had to do was fall into place and treat him with the same unquestioning deference as everyone else.

He'd hurt her and she was supposed to forgive.

Instead of which he'd hurt her and she'd hurt him right back. And now she was back here and they were hurting each other again and she wanted it to stop as quickly as humanely possible. 'I should never have come and you shouldn't have put us all in this position. Why on earth did you insist on having me as maid of honour?'

'Because you're my best friend. We've been best friends since we bonded over the grim accommodation at college. Your room was bigger than mine. I needed access to the space.'

Best friends forever.

'You choose the oddest moments to be soppy.' Laurel stood stiff. Just because her friendship with

Dani meant everything to her didn't mean she could articulate her feelings.

'You don't give your love easily but when you do it's forever. I know how much you loved Cristiano.' Like an interrogator, Dani advanced on her. 'Every time we've seen each other over the past two years you've dodged this issue, but I'm not letting you dodge it now. I want to know what went wrong. Give me details.'

Somehow Laurel made her lips move. 'I left.'

'Yes, but *why*?' Dani took her hands and hesitated. 'Cristiano told me that you had a miscarriage. Don't be mad at him for telling me. I *made* him tell me what had happened. I just wish you'd called me.'

'There was nothing you could have done.'

'I could have listened. You must have been devastated.'

Devastated. Did that word begin to describe what she'd felt that day?

Dani's hands tightened on hers. 'You must have felt dreadful. But I can't believe you walked out because of that. I just can't. Did he say something? Do something?'

He'd done nothing. Absolutely nothing.

Not even interrupted his meeting.

It was typical of sweet, sensitive Dani to guess that her brother wasn't blameless but the last thing Laurel needed or wanted was reconciliation.

She wasn't punishing him or sulking. She was protecting herself.

And she'd carry on protecting herself because that was what she had always done.

'I know what men are like.' Dani refused to give up, as stubborn as her brother in many ways. 'Mostly insensitive, with a huge streak of ego. They invariably say the wrong thing and if we get upset about it they accuse us of overreacting or being hormonal. Sometimes I could strangle Raimondo.'

'You're marrying him tomorrow.'

'Because I love him and I'm training him to not be an insufferable jerk. Cristiano is my brother but that doesn't make me blind to his faults. Maybe we're all to blame because we depend on him so much.' Dani let go of Laurel's hands. 'When Dad died it was a hideous time. Mum was a mess—I was just eleven, Santo was still at school. Cristiano flew home from the States and took charge. And we all leaned on him—' she pulled a face '—and we've been doing it ever since. Because he turned Dad's dream into reality, this hugely successful global business employing thousands, everyone thinks he walks on water, but I do see how stubborn and arrogant he can be. Tell me what he did to you, Laurie. Was it the whole "taking charge" thing? That always drives me mad.'

Laurel's heart was hammering. 'I appreciate what you're trying to do here, Dani, but it isn't going to change anything. It's finished. We can't go back. And I wouldn't want to.'

'You were perfect together. So perfect it was actually a bit sickening to watch, to be honest. But it gave the rest of us faith that love really does exist. Even cynical Santo was shocked by the change in Cristiano. We'd never heard him laugh so much.'

Feeling like a fish on a hook, Laurel glared at her friend. 'We barely knew each other when we got married.' But she'd taken that chance. Allowed herself to live for the moment. 'It's no good you trying to turn this into a fairy tale, Dani. There is no fairy tale. I can't help that you want it to be something different. Not every episode of hot sex ends in a happy ever after.'

Daniela's dark eyes brimmed with tears of distress and frustration. 'You and Cristiano should be together.'

'Is that why you refused to meet me at the airport? So that we'd be thrown together? You don't know what you're doing.' Laurel felt cornered. 'You have to stop meddling. A lot of people could end up hurt.'

'People *are* hurt, Laurel! My brother is in agony and I have to stand by and watch him being all strong, and I *know* you're hurting too—' tears slid down her face and Dani swore softly as she wiped them away with the palm of her hand '—and now I'm going to ruin my make-up. We're not going to be able to have photographs at the wedding at this rate. Laurel, for God's sake, whatever the hell happened, just forgive each other and move on.'

'I am moving on. I've moved on.'

'I mean with him, not without him.'

Laurel was tired of fighting. 'It was wrong of you to interfere. Wrong of you to put us in the same villa—cruel—'

'When you were together before, the two of you couldn't keep your hands off each other—' Dani blew her nose. 'I thought maybe if you were trapped together you might be able to sort it out.'

'Well, we can't.' She should have known this couldn't work. The Ferrara family were like chain mail—all intertwined and linked together into a strong whole. 'I'll leave first thing tomorrow. I shouldn't have come.'

'You're my maid of honour! I want you here for my wedding.'

Laurel looked at her in frustration. 'My being here is tearing this family apart.' And it was tearing her apart. Being this close to Cristiano was far, far more painful than she ever could have imagined possible. The pain of it was a dull, throbbing ache that nothing would ease.

'*Don't* leave!'

'We're not eighteen any more. A lot has changed.' Laurel stood rigidly, wondering when her friend had become so selfish that she only thought about her own needs. Being here was killing her. 'You have your little cousins as attendants.' Four dark-haired minxes who were running round creating havoc beneath them, enchanting everyone with their unselfconscious enjoyment of the party.

'I want *you*, and I want you and Cristiano back together.'

Some might have called Dani shallow, but Laurel envied the fact that her polished view of the world had never been tarnished. *That she still believed good things happened to good people.*

'There's a party in your honour going on downstairs. We should go down.' She eased herself out of her friend's embrace and this time Dani didn't resist.

Laurel remembered all the times they'd giggled together in their student rooms and had a sudden yearning for the simplicity of those days.

Some people thought it was better to have loved and lost than never to have loved at all.

Laurel thought they were mad.

CHAPTER THREE

EXHAUSTED from the emotional bombardment, Laurel wondered whether she'd survive an entire evening within touching distance of Cristiano. It had been so long since she'd spent time with him she felt like an addict starved of a fix.

From across the terrace she heard him laugh and she turned her head, drawn by the sound. She'd never laughed as much as she had when they were together. Life had felt light and full of hope. Now he was laughing with another woman.

And she was beautiful.

There was an intimacy in the way they communicated, an ease that suggested a relationship deeper than friendship.

Torturing herself, Laurel was unable to drag her eyes away. As she watched, one of the little cousins dressed in a froth of blue danced across to him and tugged at his leg. With an indulgent smile, Cristiano scooped her up and gave her his full attention. Laurel couldn't hear what he was saying but, judging from the child's expression, it was something amusing.

His interaction with the child was enough to unlock everything trapped inside her.

Laurel turned away, wondering if anyone would notice if she slipped away.

It didn't matter where she stood, she was aware of him. Even with her back to him she could sense him. The feeling crept over her skin and took control of her mind, making it impossible to concentrate on a conversation. Her neck ached with the need to turn and look. For once she was grateful for the crowd of people and the constraints of social behaviour that prevented her from rushing across to his side and undoing everything she'd done.

'You should eat something.' He appeared by her side, cool and commanding as he gestured towards one of the waitresses circulating with a tray of canapés.

'I'm not hungry.'

Cristiano took a small piece of chicken from the plate. 'Unless you're trying to draw attention to yourself, I suggest you eat. It's marinated in local lemon juice and herbs. Your favourite.'

She wondered if he was doing it on purpose, conjuring up shared memories of the night they'd raided the kitchen like children and taken food down to the beach.

That decadent moonlit picnic was one of her happiest memories of their time together.

Feeling as if she might choke on the sadness, Laurel took the chicken because it seemed easier than arguing and it gave her something to do. Somehow she managed to chew and swallow, despite the lump in her throat and the fact he was watching her with those dark, velvety eyes that saw too much.

She looked away from the cynical curve of his mouth, shaken by the impulse that washed over her. Standing as close as they were, it would take no effort to press her lips to his. She would melt into him and then his hands would be in her hair, his mouth devouring hers with a skill that would leave her head spinning. No one kissed like Cristiano. He had an innate understanding of what a woman needed and his repertoire ranged from hot and out of control to slow and sensuous. He'd introduced her to a whole world she'd never known about.

The scent of the sea mingled with the sweetness of Mediterranean flowers and from all around them came the clink of glasses and the hum of conversation. The terrace was crowded with people and yet it might as well have been just the two of them.

His eyes darkened under the veil of those thick lashes and the atmosphere between them shifted. To the casual onlooker they were just two people in the middle of a polite conversation, but Laurel felt the sudden change as clearly as he did. The fact that it was subtle made it no less dangerous.

It was as if she were in a tiny boat being drawn by the current towards a lethal waterfall. Frantic, she tried to pull back mentally—to save herself before she plunged.

'I heard that you and Santo have finally found a prime piece of land in Sardinia.' Her carefully chosen reminder of his unwavering commitment to the business had the desired effect.

His beautiful eyes narrowed warily. 'We're negotiating a deal on the land now. Developing in Sardinia isn't easy.'

But he'd find a way.

This was what he did. He relished the challenge, if only to prove that he could outsmart and outwit the opposition.

That was why he was so angry with her, she mused. It wasn't just that she'd left. It was because she hadn't given him the opportunity to fight and win a victory. She'd just retreated.

'Congratulations. I know how much you wanted to expand there.'

'The deal isn't done yet.'

But it would be.

She had no doubt about that.

The silence sizzled with undercurrents but the presence of so many guests meant that their interaction could be nothing but civilized. She was aware of the curiosity of the crowd but Cristiano wielded too much power and influence for anyone to dare to stare or openly speculate.

Suddenly she wondered if their separation had been hard for him, this man who had lived such a gilded existence. His life was an upward trajectory, soaring higher and higher. Until she'd walked out, his ambitions for the future had continued unimpeded.

'This is where you've been hiding, Cristiano.' The scent of flowers surrendered to the stronger smell of perfume as another beautiful girl approached, this one with sloe eyes and a wide, sensuous mouth. That mouth curved into a smile that was unmistakably flirtatious and she didn't glance once in Laurel's direction as she placed a proprietorial hand on his arm.

Laurel was shocked by the flash of jealousy that consumed her.

She stared at that hand, consumed by a sick feeling that came with witnessing such a blatant act of possession. The long red nails reminded her of splashes of blood. It couldn't have hurt more if the girl had dug them straight into Laurel's heart.

Jealousy became a fizz of anger.

They never left him alone. Wherever they went, women elbowed each other to get closer, to flirt, to attract his attention, to try and take a piece of him.

And he didn't consider it strange because this had been his experience for all of his adult life.

She still remembered the shock on his face when he'd asked her out and she'd turned him down.

Almost as great as his shock when she'd walked out on their marriage.

Driven to the edge of her tolerance by those long red nails and that look of promise, Laurel turned to walk away but Cristiano was faster. With a smooth, decisive movement, his hand shot out and he closed his fingers around her wrist, preventing her escape with a grip as secure as any handcuff. 'Adele, I don't believe you've met Laurel.'

'Oh.' The girl's smile slipped slightly, her cool response revealing just where Laurel ranked in her list of influential social contacts. 'Hi.'

'My wife,' Cristiano said in a firm voice and the smile vanished altogether.

Laurel stood still, aware only of the blood pounding in her ears and his iron hold on her wrist.

It was too little, too late and she didn't understand it.

Why would he emphasize a relationship that was over?

The girl's eyes narrowed slightly and her hand slipped from Cristiano's arm. 'Ah. I'm sure you two have lots to talk about.' With a smile at Laurel that clearly said, *I can wait until you're off the scene*, the girl sashayed away to talk to Santo, who was laughing at the far end of the terrace.

'You see?' His voice was harsh. 'I *can* be sensitive.' It was a blatant reference to the occasion when she'd lost her cool, upset by the continuous stream of women who seemed to consider a wife no impediment to flirtation. She'd accused him of insensitivity. He'd accused her of overreacting.

For him to finally acknowledge her feelings on the subject only when they were this close to divorce bordered on the *insensitive*, she thought numbly. All he'd done was prove that he could have made the effort if he'd wanted to.

'I no longer care who flirts with you.' She wanted that to be true, but her mind had other ideas and tortured her with questions about which of the girls Cristiano was seeing. Because of course he had to be seeing someone. It had been two years. A man like him wasn't going to be on his own for long once word got around that his wife had left him.

'Do you expect me to believe that?' He took absolutely no notice of the women glancing at him across the sunlit terrace. Soon the sun would fade and the twinkling bulbs wound around the trees would send sparkles of light across the water. It was a breathtakingly romantic setting, the beauty of the surroundings a cruel backdrop for playing out the final scenes of a dying marriage.

'I don't really care if you believe it. I'm not saying it to challenge you.' Did he realise that he was still holding her wrist? And why wasn't she pulling her arm away? Across the terrace the dark-haired girl was holding court, every exaggerated toss of her head designed to draw the attention of the only man who interested her. 'I really don't care if you have yourself a harem.'

'Would it make you feel better if I had? Ease your conscience?' They were standing close to each other, his hand still locked on her arm in a proprietorial gesture that made no sense.

'I have nothing on my conscience.'

She knew from the sudden defensive flash in his eyes that he'd picked up her implication that his own conscience was the one that should be hurting. No one could accuse Cristiano Ferrara of being slow. His mind was as sharp as a blade.

Which made his refusal to apologise all the more hurtful.

He breathed deeply and she wondered whether this was the moment he'd finally admit his contribution to their break up. 'We stood together in the little chapel that has been part of my family's estate for generations, and I made you a promise. For better, for worse. In sickness and in health.' His anger was no less dangerous for the fact that it was so ruthlessly contained. 'You made the same promises. You were wearing a pretty white dress at the time—lace at the neck and my grandmother's antique veil. Remember? Is this ringing any bells in that messed up head of yours?'

The memory felled her at the knees and was the only reason she didn't slap him for his inability to see his own part in their break up. 'You are accusing me of breaking promises? *In sickness and in health,* Cristiano.' In that small intimate space they'd created, she threw his words back at him. 'Nowhere in our marriage vows did it say, *Just as long as neither interferes with your husband's business deals.*'

Furious with herself for opening up a wound she'd wanted to keep closed and even more furious with him for being so blind to his own shortcomings, Laurel thrust her glass into his hand, twisted free and virtually sprinted across the terrace towards the steps that led down to the private beach. She felt like Cinderella on the dot of midnight, except that she didn't want the Prince to catch her.

She could lose both shoes for all she cared. That wouldn't be enough to stop her running.

Santo stepped in front of her, his expression deceptively benign as he blocked her path. 'Where do you think you're going?'

Laurel ground her teeth, silently cursing everyone with the surname Ferrara. 'Back to the villa. Not that it's your business.'

'You're hurting my brother. That makes it my business.'

'He's big enough to look after himself.' But that

wouldn't stop Santo and her insides twisted with envy because she knew he was just looking out for his brother.

The fact that no one looked out for her didn't bother her.

She didn't expect it or want it. Never had.

'Having you here messes with his head. I just want to say one thing, Laurel—' Three parts drunk, ten parts angry, Santo blocked the steps. 'Hurt my brother again and I will crush you like a bug. *Capisci?*'

'*Non capisce niente,*' Laurel shot back, her Italian almost as fluent as his. 'You understand nothing. Stay out of my business, Santo.'

Hurt my brother—

What about the way his brother had hurt *her*? Apparently that counted for nothing.

Distress breaking through the barriers she'd erected, she pushed past him, aware that by doing so she'd made herself the object of curious stares. Doubtless everyone wanted to know what Santo had been saying to his brother's disobedient ex-wife to make her run.

She virtually flew down the steps that led down to the beach. At some point while she'd been suffering on the terrace, darkness had fallen and the solar-powered lights that illuminated the path down to the beach glowed like a million bright eyes watching her flee. Feeling her chest tighten ominously, she slowed her pace. The last thing she needed right now was an asthma attack. She was ruthless about maintaining her fitness levels but her downfall had always been stress and she'd been stressed from the moment the wheels of the plane had touched the tarmac.

As her feet sank into the soft sand the chatter behind her faded and the music became a distant hum. Here, the dominant sound was the lap of the sea on the shore and Laurel tugged off her shoes. The solitude was a soothing balm to her raw feelings, the silky sand triggering memories of happier times. But memories couldn't change the present.

They were all furious with her. She was about as welcome as a deadly virus at a children's party.

And she was furious with *them* for assuming that all the blame lay with her.

She was here because of Dani, but it was clear to her now that once her friend accepted that Laurel and Cristiano really were finished, their friendship would be over too.

Depressed by that thought, Laurel sank down onto the sand and wrapped her arms around her knees, her bag and her shoes abandoned by her side. The sea stretched ahead of her, the inky black broken by the occasional shimmer of light from a passing yacht.

She'd been stupid, she realised, to think that her

friendship with Dani could endure, given what she'd done.

Desperately she struggled to control herself, aware that her chest was growing tighter and doing everything she could to breathe slowly and keep herself calm.

She didn't know how long she sat there staring through a mist of tears, but she knew when she was no longer alone.

Infuriated that he didn't have the sensitivity to leave her alone, she tensed her shoulders. 'Go back to the party, Cristiano. We have nothing more to talk about.' The moon sent a shaft of light over the sea, illuminating the hard, masculine features.

'I want to talk about the baby.'

So he'd been saving the worst for last. 'I don't.'

'I know, and that's why we're in this mess. Because you refused to talk about it.'

The injustice of it knocked the last of the breath from her lungs.

Even now, broaching this most delicate of topics, his body language had all the subtlety of one of the many invaders who had plundered Sicily for two thousand years of its colourful history.

His legs were planted firmly apart, one hand in his pocket, indifferent to the effects of the sand on the sheen of his designer shoes. Laurel recognised the stance. This was Cristiano troubleshooting, those broad shoulders set for battle and those charcoal eyes narrowed to two dangerous slits as he assessed the opposition and realigned his strategy.

He was six foot two of furiously angry Sicilian male, ready to fight until victory was his.

And even as part of her loathed that side of him, another part admired that strength and focus.

Telling herself that raw masculinity was just not attractive, she gritted her teeth.

Kill it right now, Laurel. Those tiny, dangerous shoots of desire needed to be culled before they spread and threatened to choke common sense.

'You want to talk about the baby? Fine—let's talk. I was ten weeks pregnant. I had abdominal cramps. You were away on business. I called you, but you decided it would be fine to carry on with your business trip. You made your decision. Things became worse. I called you again but you'd switched your phone off. You couldn't have been clearer about your priorities. There's nothing more to be said on the subject.' The idyllic setting did nothing to dilute the tension that throbbed between them.

'You are twisting the facts. I called the doctor. I spoke to him and he assured me that with a few days' rest you would be all right. No one expected you to lose the baby.'

She'd expected to lose the baby. From the first cramp she'd known with a woman's instinct that something was badly wrong. 'Then that's you off the hook.'

'*Accidenti*, why do you refuse to discuss it?'

'Because this is not a discussion. Just another monologue where you tell me how I should be feeling. You want me to tell you that it was all my fault, that I behaved unreasonably, but I'm not going to do that because I didn't. You are the one who behaved unreasonably.' The rhythm of her breathing was unsteady. 'No, not unreasonably—that isn't the word. You were cruel, Cristiano. Cruel.'

'*Basta!* Enough.' His voice thickened around the word. 'You make it sound as if this was a straightforward decision but my role in this company comes with huge responsibilities. The decisions that I make affect thousands. And sometimes those decisions are difficult.'

'And sometimes they're just plain wrong. Admit it.'

He exhaled and swore simultaneously, exasperation and frustration etched in the perfect symmetry of his face. 'Of course, with hindsight, I admit I may have made the wrong decision that day.'

It was the closest he'd ever come to an apology but it made no difference to the raw pain inside her. Swept along in an avalanche of emotions, she forgot her promise to herself not to revisit the past. 'It shouldn't require hindsight for you to know you messed up badly. You *knew* how much it took for me to call you and ask you to come that day. When had I ever asked for your help or support before?

Never. Just that one time when I was alone and terrified. All you needed was just a gram of sensitivity but no, you were too busy playing the big tycoon. And do you know the worst thing?' Her voice shook. 'Until I met you I had never needed anyone. I was strong. I relied only on myself. I sorted my own life out. But you prised me open like a shell on a beach, removing all my protection. You demanded that I open up. You *made* me need you and stupidly I gave you that power. And then you let me down.'

Cristiano yanked at his bow tie and dragged open his top button as if it was strangling him. 'I am running a global corporation. I am a man with enormous responsibilities and on this occasion—'

'What you are, Cristiano, is a man who puts his wife second to his business interests. Do you know what really depresses me? The fact that even now you're not willing to admit you made a lousy decision. The words "I may have made the wrong decision" have to be virtually dragged from you because you don't believe yourself capable of getting anything wrong. Well, I've got news for you—you *definitely* made the wrong decision.' She flung back her head and her hair slid loose over her shoulders. Like a samurai falling on his sword, she uttered the words that she knew would kill their relationship for ever. 'And I hate you for that almost as much as I hate you for making me need you. You're an insensitive, arrogant bully and I don't want you in my life.'

'A *bully?*' Those powerful shoulders were rigid. 'So now I'm a bully?'

She noticed that he didn't challenge her on the charge of being insensitive and arrogant. 'You push and push until things go the way you want them to go. It doesn't matter what you're doing, you always have to win. When there's something you want, you develop tunnel vision. You wanted that Caribbean deal so badly you told yourself I'd be fine. You justified your behaviour by reminding yourself how many people were depending on you, that it was your responsibility to stay and finish the meeting, but the truth is that you stayed because you never think anyone can do the job as well as you and also because you love the buzz of winning. I'd have more respect for you if you were just honest enough to admit it. But you have to tell yourself it's *my* fault because the alternative is recognising your own error and you don't make errors, do you?' It was possibly the longest, most revealing speech she'd ever made to him and she saw the shock in his eyes as he registered the change in her.

In the shaft of moonlight two livid lines of colour streaked along his enviable cheekbones. 'I have already admitted I made the wrong decision. But once again you've managed to divert the conversation from the baby you lost.'

We lost, she thought numbly. *We* lost it. And as usual his answer to her suggestion of any failing on his part was to brush over it as virtually inconsequential.

'You're so proud of the fact that you talk about your feelings so easily, but they're *your* feelings, Cristiano. You have no interest in anyone else's unless they match your own. The reason you want to know my feelings is so that you can tell me I'm wrong. So that you can change my mind and tell me what I should be thinking. You have the sensitivity of a tank and I hate your macho, caveman approach to everything.'

The atmosphere snapped taut and his eyes glittered lethal black in the dim light. 'I can remember a time when you liked my macho, caveman approach.'

The sudden punch of sensual heat horrified her. 'That was a long time ago.'

'Really?' She was hauled to her feet before she could do more than gasp his name.

Unprepared and off balance, she tipped against him and was forced to plant her hand against his chest for support. Through the fine silk of his shirt she felt hard male muscle and could feel him literally vibrating with anger. His dark features loomed over her and she swayed towards him like someone in a trance. The heat was suffocating but she had no idea whether it was the sultry Sicilian air or their scorching passion that seared her skin.

Safe in another country, it had been easy to rationalise the chemistry, but the reality was raw and frightening.

Two years of self-denial weakened her still further and, instead of pushing him away, her fingers fisted in his shirt. Helpless, hopeless, she watched as his head lowered towards hers, the sheer inevitability of it melting her resistance.

She was so ready for his kiss, *so desperate*, that it was a brutal shock when he released her suddenly.

In a smooth movement he uncurled her fingers from his shirt as if she were an insect he didn't want touching his flesh. 'You're right—' he spoke in a tone thickened with contempt and disdain as he thrust her away from him '—there is no point in conversation. Nothing, *nothing*, justifies you walking away from our marriage. You think you're so tough and independent but you're a coward who would rather run than stay and fight.'

And run she did. Right then, with her feet bare and her heart exposed. She sprinted along the sand, her hair flying in her face as she ran towards the safety of the villa.

Coward, coward, coward—

Each time her feet hit the sand she heard the word in her head and she increased the pace, trying to outrun the noise.

The tightness in her chest was back but she ran without pausing, without looking back. She ran until her lungs burned and by the time she reached the villa, she could hardly breathe.

Doubled over, she paused by the door. And knew instantly that she was in trouble.

She needed the inhaler now. Right now, if she were to avoid the attack that threatened.

A few minutes before, her biggest fear had been the way she felt about him, but suddenly that fear had been surpassed by something even more dangerous. The need for air.

Her lungs burned and breathing was becoming harder and harder. With hands that shook she automatically reached for her bag, only to discover she was no longer carrying it. She'd put it down on the sand next to her and she'd forgotten to pick it up when she'd been trying to escape from Cristiano.

Laurel knew a moment of real terror and she mentally cursed herself for being so stupid. She should have used her inhaler earlier instead of arguing with him.

Her chest was growing worse by the minute. Her breathing tighter and more laboured. Knowing that she didn't have her inhaler made the stress worse.

Being on her own with an attack was something she dreaded more than anything.

Knowing that she was in serious trouble, Laurel let herself into the villa and sank down onto the floor with her back to the wall. *Breathe. Breathe.* Slowly. Relax. She needed to go back and find her inhaler but at the moment she wasn't capable of walking that far.

Telling herself that she'd be fine if she could just calm down, she forced herself to focus on the lamp glowing in the corner of the room and forget her encounter with Cristiano, but it was hard to be calm when every breath was an effort.

Her chest became tighter and she heard the whistling sound that came with the onset of an attack.

No. Not now.

The door crashed open. 'Always you run, but you and I are going to—' Cristiano broke off as he saw her huddled in the corner, struggling to breathe. In one stride he was beside her. 'Laurel?' He dropped into a crouch, his hand sliding into her hair so that he could tilt her head and look at her properly. 'Asthma?'

Wordless, she nodded.

'You're a fool, running like that. Where is your inhaler?' He displayed that same ability to focus and prioritise that had brought him staggering success in the business world. For those few crucial moments everything between them was forgotten.

'Bag—dropped it—'

'This bag?' Her tiny silver purse dangled from his fingers and her shoulders slumped with relief as she nodded. Already the wheeze was becoming worse.

Hands shaking, she reached for the bag but he

was already opening it, his movements swift and purposeful as he extracted the inhaler.

'This one?'

She nodded and his mouth tightened.

'You shouldn't have run.'

It wasn't the running that had caused it but she didn't have the air to tell him that so she simply watched as he yanked the cap off the inhaler. 'Since when has your asthma got this bad?'

Since her stress levels had gone through the roof. *Since that awful night in the hospital.*

Laurel wanted to sob but she didn't have enough air to do it and she cupped his hands gratefully as he held the inhaler to her lips. She breathed in, drawing comfort from the fact that he was there, right in front of her. Strong. Reassuring. In a minute she'd send him away, but for now—for now his hands were warm and steady, his calm a soothing balm to her anxiety.

His beautiful, sexy mouth was set in a grim line. 'I'll call a doctor.'

Laurel shook her head, breathed one more time and then pushed his hands and the inhaler away. If she could still notice that his mouth was sexy then she wasn't going to die any time soon. She leaned her head back against the wall. 'Go back to the party.'

'*Sì*, because the one thing I really feel like doing right now is dancing the night away.' But this time the sarcasm was blunted by concern as well as exasperation. 'I am a man who learns from his mistakes, *tesoro*. Last time I walked away when you needed me, although in my defence I didn't realise how bad it was—' His eyes never left hers.

'You just can't do it, can you?' Laurel took a few difficult breaths. 'You can't….apologise.'

The corners of his mouth flickered. 'For once I'm relieved you have the breath to argue. And, as for an apology—I'm getting closer by the minute.'

'Don't bother. It's too late to make a difference… I already hate you.' Laurel closed her eyes but not before she'd seen a tempting hint of bronzed skin with the cluster of dark hair hinting at what lay beneath his shirt.

It didn't help that she knew *exactly* what lay beneath. She could picture it, every tempting curve and dip of his muscles, the taut flat abdomen and the firm thighs. He was the only client she'd ever had whose physique she hadn't been able to improve.

'You don't hate me, *tesoro*.' The assurance with which he spoke those words should have angered her because she'd always hated the way he accepted people's respect and adulation as his due. He didn't just walk into a room, he commanded it and that natural assumption of power had exasperated her.

Her throat tightened again, but this time the response was nothing to do with her asthma.

'Go, or there will be gossip.'

'I'm not even going to respond to that.' His arm brushed against hers although whether by accident or design she didn't know. 'Do you need to inhale this thing again?'

She opened her eyes.

He still held her inhaler in his fingers and she shook her head.

'Maybe in a minute… And if you don't go back, Dani will notice.'

'When Dani sees that both of us are missing she'll assume we're together. She'll be opening champagne and congratulating herself.'

'That's what worries me. Go.'

'You really think I'd leave? I learned that lesson two years ago.'

The irony of it would have made her smile if she'd had the energy. 'Two years ago I wanted you—now I don't.' Her lungs were improving, the desperate fight for air eased by the medication. 'I'm not a hypocrite. I chose to leave this marriage so I can't expect you to hold my hand just because I'm scared. Not that I'm saying I'm scared.'

'Of course you're not. God forbid that you would ever admit to vulnerability. Tell me something—' his tone was conversational, as if they hadn't just been engaged in a blistering row '—have you ever leaned on anyone in your life?'

'I leaned on you.' *And you weren't there.*

Hearing those unspoken words loud and clear, his

jaw tightened. 'I asked for that one.' He sat down on the floor next to her, his broad shoulders pressed against the wall. The sleeve of his jacket brushed against her bare arm and Laurel felt the connection deep down in her soul. She hadn't expected him to stay.

'I don't remember inviting you to sit down.'

Ignoring her, he leaned his head back. 'You're the most aggravating woman I've ever met, you do know that, don't you?'

'You talk to me of aggravating?' She didn't know whether to laugh or cry. 'When I needed you most you were nowhere to be seen and now I don't need you I can't get rid of you. *That's* aggravating. Go back to your other women, Cristiano.'

'Which one? According to you, I have a harem.'

'I'm sure any one of them would provide you with the slavish adoration you need.' Laurel felt the solid warmth of his arm pressing against her. *He smelled so good,* she thought dizzily. Her senses were heightened, her skin tingling and her nerve endings buzzing. Recognising the danger signs, she felt a stab of alarm. She needed him to leave. Either that or *she* needed to leave but she didn't have the available breath. *Or anywhere to go.* 'Your problem is that you think women are a homogeneous group. You think we all think and feel in the same way.'

'You're wasting precious breath spouting rubbish.'

'You think we're an inferior species.'

He threw back his head and laughed at that. 'Is that the best you can do to pick a fight? Now I know you're feeling bad.'

'I just want you to go.'

'*Sì*, I know.' His voice was low and rough. 'But I'm not going anywhere.'

'I find it stressful you being here.'

It was a moment before he answered. 'Why?'

The sounds of the night intruded on the silence. The rhythmic chirruping of the cicadas and the soft swish of sea on sand. Romance intruding where it had no business.

'A million reasons.'

The tension pulsed between them and Laurel pressed her hands to the ground, intending to lever herself away from him, but his hand clamped over hers.

'Name one.'

'Because our marriage is over. And because you always want everything your own way. There, I gave you two.' She tugged, but he was stronger. 'Let me go. My legs are numb. I need to move.'

'Of course you do. Whenever the conversation becomes uncomfortable you want to move. Usually as fast as possible in the opposite direction.' He levered himself to his feet. 'I'll allow you to go as far as the bed.' Without giving her the opportunity to argue, he scooped her into his arms.

'Oh, for goodness' sake—I can walk. I don't need

all this macho stuff. I've told you, it does nothing for me.' Her breathing felt strange again but this time she knew it had nothing to do with her asthma and everything to do with being this close to him. She wrapped her arms around his neck, telling herself it was just for support. Nothing else.

The doors were open to the beach and a slight breeze cooled the air as he laid her gently on the bed.

He removed his jacket and slung it carelessly over the sofa. Then he piled the pillows up behind her. 'Better?' At her reluctant nod his mouth tightened. 'When did your asthma become this bad? In all the time we were together I only saw you have an attack once and that was when my pilot had to make an emergency landing and some fool told you about it.'

She didn't even want to think about the terror of that day. Not now, when she was working on forgetting what they'd shared in the past. 'You and I were in the middle of a huge project. I didn't want you dying and leaving me with all the work.'

The corners of his mouth tilted in appreciative humour. 'Of course. You were worried about the workload. It wasn't because I rocked your world.'

'I didn't see enough of you for you to rock my world. At the most you were a faint tremble.'

'So if I had so little impact on your life, why did you pack two inhalers to come to this wedding?'

'Are there two in my bag?' She feigned surprise and his lashes swept down over his eyes, concealing his expression, but not before she'd seen the flash of exasperation.

'I wish you would learn to be honest about your feelings.'

'I wish you would learn not to let your feelings spill out. I suppose I have to make allowances for the fact you're Sicilian.'

'Allowances?'

It was a relief to know she could still irritate him. Two minutes, she thought, and then he'd be ranting in Italian and storming out. *She was relying on it.* 'Being Sicilian is a handicap in life,' she murmured sympathetically. 'Being emotional is welded into your DNA. You can't help it.'

'Not everyone is afraid of emotions.' He undid the cuffs of his shirt in a slow, deliberate movement. 'But you are. Terrified. Two-inhalers terrified.'

She wondered why he was removing his jacket when what he should really be doing was redoing his bow tie and returning to the party.

When she remained silent he raised an eyebrow and dropped his cufflinks onto the small writing table that faced the sea. 'What, no comeback, Laurel? No incendiary statement designed to make me walk out? That's what you want, isn't it? Do you think I don't know that?' The sleeves of his shirt flopped over his strong hands and he folded them back and pushed them up his arms. She remembered those arms holding her and immediately looked away, rejecting the powerful surge of need. She'd always found it unfair that someone with such a casual attitude to his appearance could look so good in every situation.

'You can stay or go, I don't care. I don't need you.'

'Need and want are two different things.' He looked at the inhaler clutched in her palm. 'So your attacks are brought on by stress. That's interesting. You weren't stressed when we were together.'

'As I said, that's because I never saw you,' she said sweetly. 'I've seen more of you in the last twenty-four hours than I ever did during our marriage. Probably why I'm stressed.'

'I'm stressed too. You are enough to drive a man crazy.' His low drawl connected with her insides and suddenly that melting feeling low in her pelvis was back.

'You only have to survive my company until Sunday. My flight leaves first thing in the morning.'

'We have a meeting with the lawyers tomorrow morning.'

'I don't need to speak to them. Agree whatever you want and it will be fine by me.'

The mattress moved as he sat down next to her. 'If you're that angry with me then this is your chance to bleed me dry.'

'It was never about the money, you know that.'

'I don't know anything because you never share anything. A relationship with you is one big guessing game.' He sounded tired and witnessing that was a thousand times more unsettling than his anger or sarcasm because she'd never seen him tired. Cristiano had more energy than any man she'd ever met.

'If you'd been around more you wouldn't have had to guess.' On that terrible day—*the day he'd missed*—her feelings had been there for all to see. Except the only witnesses had been the staff of the private hospital. Competent but brisk, they'd had no idea of the extent of her desolation. 'I'll fly home tomorrow. The last thing you need right now is your ex-wife at your sister's wedding.'

'Wife.' The words were soft but firm. 'You're not my *ex*-wife.'

'Soon will be.' It was so dangerous, being this close to him. She didn't dare look at him. Didn't dare move in case she brushed against him, so she held herself rigid.

'Your breathing is better.'

'So now you can go back to the party.'

He didn't rise but he did give her a warning look. 'I'll sleep on the sofa in the living room. Leave the door open. If you need anything you can call out.'

A lump settled in her throat. 'Honestly, you don't need to do this. Just go and answer the thousands of emails that will undoubtedly be waiting for you on your phone.' *She didn't want him to behave decently now. It was too late.*

'So now you're giving me permission to be insensitive?'

Yes, because anything different would complicate her feelings and she didn't want that.

Her mind was straight. She wanted it to stay straight.

Laurel gave a shrug that was supposed to indicate that she didn't care what he did. 'If acting like a guard dog makes you feel better about yourself then at least let me be the one to sleep on the sofa.'

'Why? I can sleep anywhere, you know that.'

She did know. In the middle of tough negotiations there had been nights when he'd slept in the office to avoid coming home in the middle of the night and waking her. 'In that case, do whatever pleases you.'

When he reached out to switch off the lamp by the bed she caught his arm. 'Leave it.'

It was such a cliché, but she hated the dark.

On her own, she always slept with a light on. Only with Cristiano had she been able to feel safe at night.

He frowned, his gaze steady and disturbingly perceptive. 'I'll stay with you for a few minutes, just until I'm sure you don't need a doctor.' As he pulled off his shoes and settled on the bed next to her she wanted to ask why he was doing this. Why he was he staying with her when they were no longer together. *When it was much, much too late for their marriage.*

They sat together in silence, close but not touching. As her breathing grew easier and the panic lessened, so her awareness of him grew. The length of his powerful thigh next to hers and his deep, even breathing. The connection between them, that dangerous indefinable chemistry that should have died along with her dreams, sprang to life.

Slowly, she turned her head and looked at him.

He turned his head too and his eyes fixed on hers.

Both should have looked away but neither of them did.

The inevitability of it was as sweet and sharp as the desire that stabbed through her body.

His hand lifted and his fingers dragged lightly over her jaw. The stroke of his thumb over her lower lip was gentle. When he lowered his head he did it slowly, as if he wasn't sure he was actually going to follow through. His mouth brushed against hers. A teasing prelude. It was insane and she should have moved, but she couldn't. Anticipation exploded inside her. For a few thrilling seconds his mouth hovered close to hers and then he lost his grip on control and took her mouth in a hard, devouring kiss that blew every thought from her brain. She tried to hold herself back, not to become involved, but his kiss drew her in until they merged, until she couldn't tell where she ended and he began, until her whole world centred on what they became together. His tongue was in her mouth, his hands in her hair and they feasted on each other like animals driven wild by deprivation. It was intoxicating, the rush of sexual excitement as heady as any drug and just as dangerous.

Time passed unnoticed and then he gave a growl of self-denial and dragged his mouth from hers, regret visible in every plane of his handsome face. *'No.'* The raw emotion in his voice reflected her own feelings.

'No.' The kiss had shaken her and it was no consolation to know it had shaken him too. This wasn't what she wanted. She wasn't trying to tempt him back. She wasn't trying to instigate a reconciliation.

Her future didn't include him and yet now everything was stirred up inside her. And even while she was cursing herself a tiny rogue part of her was thrilled at the fact he'd given in to temptation because she knew he exercised ruthless control over his impulses. She'd *wanted* this encounter to be difficult for him but what they'd just done had made it a thousand times more difficult for herself.

Laurel pulled away, dizzy with the contradictory thoughts that fought for supremacy in her head. She didn't want him to want her. She didn't want to want *him.* How was that going to help? It was just going to make an already difficult situation worse.

Cristiano sprang from the bed, lithe and supremely fit. 'You're right. I should sleep on the sofa. If you need a doctor in the night, call me.' With that terse instruction and not even a glance in her direction, he left the room, leaving her body buzzing and her heart breaking.

CHAPTER FOUR

'CRISTIANO, are you even listening to me?'

Cristiano turned, disconcerted to realise he hadn't heard a single word his lawyer had spoken.

He'd left the villa at sunrise, attempting to relieve his rocketing tension levels with a punishing run before the warmth of the new day turned to blistering heat. After that, he'd swum. Then he'd caught up on his emails.

Nothing had deleted thoughts of Laurel from his brain.

He wanted to see her as the heartless bitch who had treated their marriage vows as nothing but instead he kept seeing her, pale and vulnerable as she struggled to breathe, stressed out of her mind by being back with him. Accustomed to handling a variety of emergencies on an everyday basis, he'd been appalled by the panic that had gripped him witnessing her struggle for air. He'd been perilously close to summoning every doctor on the island.

Every doctor except the idiot who had assured

him that it was common for a woman to have abdominal cramps and that it was unlikely she'd lose the baby.

Anger shafted through him, but the strongest emotion was one of guilt as he acknowledged the damage he'd done by choosing to prioritise a critical work issue over her well-being. The fact that he'd grossly underestimated the seriousness of the situation didn't excuse him. The fact that the advice of another had proved ill-founded didn't excuse him either.

His mind was full of questions, the answers to which should have been of no interest or relevance at this stage of their relationship. He wanted to know since when her asthma had been that bad. Whether she'd been having attacks in the time they had been apart. He knew she'd suffered since childhood. It was one of the few things she'd told him about herself when they'd first met.

He knew that, for her, stress was the trigger.

If last night was anything to go by, she was under monumental stress.

Acknowledging the part his own behaviour had played in the onset of her attack, Cristiano ran his hand over his face. He couldn't believe his own lack of control. From the moment he'd met her at the airport, his temper had been simmering dangerously. The relationship was over. It had been over for the past two years and yet the moment he'd seen her again the only thought in his mind had been, *She's my wife. Mine.*

Until he'd met Laurel he'd considered himself to be a modern male—well, as modern as a Sicilian man could be. The past twenty-four hours had forced a stark rethink of that overly generous self-analysis. Every dark primitive thought that had haunted his brain had taken him right back to his caveman ancestors. Jealous? Yes, he was jealous. Jealous as hell and the knowledge sat in his gut like some thick, sickening poison slowly seeping through his body, contaminating every thought.

He didn't want her moving on.

He didn't want her making a new life that didn't feature him as a central character.

His lawyer cleared his throat and pushed a file across the table to him. 'I emailed you a document. The fact that you refused to declare a separation of assets on your marriage or a pre-nuptial agreement theoretically leaves you exposed.'

'I don't care about the money.'

'Well, you're lucky. Apparently neither does she.' Carlo pulled another set of documents out of his briefcase. 'Her lawyer has said that if we can expedite the divorce proceedings, she is happy to walk away with nothing.'

The evidence that she was prepared to sacrifice anything and everything to get away from him exposed another layer of his base masculine instincts. *Did she hate him that much?* 'What did you tell him?'

'Her.' Carlo flicked through the pages until he found the one he wanted. 'Her lawyer is a woman. And I told her that in Sicily a couple have to have been separated for three years. Today is really just a formality. An opportunity to talk in person, given that you haven't seen each other for two years.'

Talk?

When had they talked? Cristiano rubbed his fingers over his forehead but nothing relieved the ugly throb in his head. He'd hurled recriminations at her and she'd reacted in her usual way—erecting more walls and barriers between them. She deflected everything he threw at her.

Her passionate accusation that he'd demanded that she open up and trust him, only to abandon her when she needed him still echoed in his brain.

He *had* let her down. But did that excuse her decision to walk out on their marriage? Not in his book.

Trying to escape from the uncomfortable throb of his own thoughts, Cristiano strode over to the window. Why, when there were millions of women who couldn't stop talking about themselves and their feelings, had he picked the one woman who refused to do either?

He knew that the miscarriage had devastated her and yet she resolutely refused to talk about it.

Perhaps the initial error had been his, but she'd shown no inclination to forgive him or accept any of his conciliatory gestures. Flowers, diamonds— she'd been too busy packing her suitcase to look at them.

His behaviour had been bad, but was it unforgivable?

'Laurel sent a message that she couldn't make this meeting because she's helping Dani—' Carlo was obviously trying to be tactful '—but I'll get the papers to her for her signature at some point today.'

Interrupting a wedding for a divorce.

The irony of it didn't escape him. He'd already briefed his pilot to be ready to fly him to Sardinia as soon as he could reasonably extricated himself. But first he had to get through the ordeal of his sister's wedding. And so did Laurel.

He hoped she had more inhalers packed in her suitcase because if stress was the trigger then she was going to need them.

He turned, feeling less in control than he would have liked. 'Do what needs to be done. I have to go and play ringmaster to this circus.'

Carlo's lips twitched. 'When I saw the flowers and the little white ponies I thought I'd stepped into a fairy tale. It's typical Dani.'

'My sister is obsessed with happy ever afters.' But Laurel wasn't. She didn't believe in happy ever afters. He still remembered how, during their wedding, she'd kept touching him to check it was real. His hand. His face. *Tell me this is happening. That I'm not going to wake up.*

For a brief moment he'd never seen anyone so happy and it had given him a real high to know that he was the one who had won her trust. A high, quickly followed by a stomach-swooping low when it had all gone so badly wrong.

For Laurel the ending hadn't been happy.

It had been one gigantic car crash.

'It fits perfectly.' Dani stood back and studied Laurel. 'You look beautiful.'

'We both know I am nowhere close to beautiful but thanks anyway. You, however, *do* look beautiful, which is a good job given that you're the bride.' Laurel smiled and fussed over her friend, hiding her pain behind activity. 'You're the one everyone is looking at.' Thank goodness. The truth was she didn't want to be wearing this pale silk sheath and carrying a small posy of sunny yellow gerberas. Not only did they not match her mood, but they reminded her too much of her own wedding. A day she was desperately trying to push from her memory.

She and Cristiano had married in the private chapel that had been in the Ferrara family for centuries. They'd married on a rush of impulse and a breathless tumble of happiness.

Dani had opted for a wedding on the beach attended, it seemed, by half the population of Sicily.

Laurel was relieved that this wedding was going to be so dramatically different from hers. There would be nothing to trigger uncomfortable memories. No nostalgia here. She just needed to get through it and go home.

Fortunately Cristiano had left the villa before she'd woken, which had spared them both another agonizing encounter. But now she was dreading the moment when she laid eyes on him again. He seemed determined to rake over the past and she had no wish to do that.

And as for that kiss—

So the man could kiss. That didn't change anything.

A kiss wasn't love.

Hands not entirely steady, she adjusted Dani's veil. 'Are you ready?'

'Oh, yes. You?'

Never. Laurel smiled. 'Absolutely. Let's do it.' *Let's get it over with, then I can go home.* Her flight was booked for the next day. All she had to do was survive the wedding, the dinner and one more night in the villa.

She would concentrate on her friend. She wasn't going to look at Cristiano.

If she needed distraction then she'd think about the fitness programme she was putting together for a client struggling with her weight. The woman had suffered serious health problems and it had been a challenge to devise a programme that would gradually build her strength without putting too much stress on her body.

It was the part of the job she loved most. Helping people grow fitter. Improving their lives. Showing them that they could make good choices.

She walked towards the door but Dani caught her arm. 'Wait for me. I want to be there to see Cristiano's face when he first sees you in that dress.'

'You never give up, do you?'

'Not when something is worth fighting for. I know you still love him.'

The words jolted Laurel out of her self-imposed semi-trance. 'Move, or you're going to be late for your own wedding.'

'Don't change the subject.'

'This is *your* wedding day! You're the subject.' She wasn't in love with him. Definitely not. It was always going to be an emotional time. That short lapse last night didn't mean anything.

'But—'

'You're keeping the groom waiting.'

As Laurel walked with Dani across the flower-strewn terrace, she had reason to be grateful for her friend's flamboyant style. Her own wedding had been small and intimate. An exchange of vows between two lovers and their closest friends and family. Dani had opted to make her wedding as big a party as possible and at least two hundred guests were seated on the enormous terrace that overlooked the beach.

Laurel stooped and rearranged the generous folds of her friend's dress, noticing with some relief that her fingers were now completely steady.

She had no idea what Cristiano's reaction to her dress was because she wasn't looking at him when he strode onto the terrace and she had plenty of reasons to keep herself otherwise occupied as he carried out his responsibilities as head of the family.

The only slightly rocky moment came when Laurel found herself face to face with his mother.

'You are back.' Not even the hot Sicilian sun could make up for the lack of warmth and Laurel knew exactly why she was being subjected to disapproval.

To Francesca Ferrara, a woman who could trace her lineage right back to the fifteenth century and earlier, Laurel must have been the daughter-in-law from hell. A mongrel, who had failed to fulfil that most basic requirement of a good Sicilian wife— turning a blind eye to her husband's bad behaviour.

'I'm back just for the wedding. Then I'm leaving.'

Fortunately, at that moment the string quartet started playing and the ceremony began, sparing Laurel an awkward conversation.

Relieved, she focused on her role as maid of honour. It was impossible not to be aware that people were looking at her, but she concentrated her attention on her friend, allowing the faces around her to blur.

As Dani spoke her vows and took Raimondo's hand, a lump formed in Laurel's throat.

Hadn't she done the same at her own wedding? She'd been so blissfully happy, so convinced that this couldn't possibly be happening to her, that she'd had to check it was real. The priest had been shocked but Cristiano had just laughed and immediately lifted back her veil and cupped her face in his strong hands, the warmth of his kiss giving her all the reassurance she'd needed.

It was that uncanny ability to see into her mind and knock aside her reservations and caution that had given depth to their relationship. He was the first man she'd allowed into her heart. The only man.

It had made the fall all the harder.

Thinking of it brought the tightness back to her chest.

A wave of dizziness rushed over her, although whether it was the intense heat of the sun or just misery she didn't know.

It was only when she became aware that Santo was staring at her intently that she realised that her cheeks were damp.

Oh, no…

Frantically trying to work out how the tears had

managed to fall without her permission, she saw the exact moment Santo's hostile stare turn to a puzzled frown.

Laurel ignored him and concentrated on her friend, desperately hoping that Cristiano hadn't witnessed her lapse in control. There was no way she dared risk a glance at him so she just had to hope he wasn't looking in her direction. And if he was— well, she'd have to pretend she had something in her eye. Sand? An insect?

Furious with herself, she stared straight forward. She wasn't a crier. Never had been. So why was it that since she'd arrived in Sicily that was all she'd felt like doing?

Maybe it was the stupid dress.

She'd spent hours planning her wardrobe, making sure that her clothes were practical. And here she was standing in the most romantic-looking dress she could have imagined witnessing a public display of love when *love* was a word she wanted to delete from her brain.

The lump in her throat grew bigger and she stood still, hardly able to breathe as her friend exchanged rings with the man she clearly adored.

Laurel wanted to cover her ears so that she didn't have to listen. And all the time she was aware of Cristiano standing in the periphery of her vision, a powerful, commanding figure in his beautifully cut dark suit.

Was he in hell, as she was? Was he suffering?
His words flew back into her head.

*We stood together in the little chapel that has
been part of my family's estate for generations, and
I made you a promise. For better, for worse. In sickness and in health... Remember?*

Oh, yes, she remembered. Every word, every
promise, was carved into her heart.

Her unhappiness felt too big for her body and
Laurel gripped her flowers tightly, trying desperately to stop her feelings from bursting out. She
willed Dani and Raimondo to hurry up so that she
could get away. She needed to do something or-
dinary. Something normal and unsentimental to
settle her emotions. She'd sneak back to the villa
and check her emails. That would bring her back to
earth. Or maybe she'd just get out of this dress and
go for a run. Lift some weights. Anything.

Desperately fighting for control, she tried to focus
on the lush gardens that surrounded the old courtyard. The air was scented with the sweet smell of
jasmine and out of the corner of her eye she caught
a flash of bright pink bougainvillea that painted the
terrace in a riot of colour. It was incredibly pretty.
The perfect place for a wedding.

Unable to help herself, she lifted her gaze to
Cristiano.

Across the terrace, their eyes met.

She wanted to look away but she didn't, and

neither did he. Couldn't? *Wouldn't?* She didn't know. All she knew was that he was looking at her as if he was trying to see into her mind, those deep-set black eyes fixed on hers as Dani and Raimondo exchanged vows.

This was us.

His lips didn't move and yet in her head she could hear him saying it.

We had this and you destroyed it.

Heart pumping, she snapped the connection and looked at Dani.

Maybe she was the one who had done the walking, but *he* was the one who'd destroyed it.

As the couple leaned forward to kiss, Laurel discovered that her skin was covered in goose bumps. What had begun as a slight trembling turned to a shiver. Sickness bloomed inside her and she felt the blood drain from her face as she witnessed their heartfelt declaration of love.

Her own emotions stripped bare, she gripped her flowers and tried to hold herself together.

The rest of the ceremony blurred into one big torture session. One big test of her self-control. She was dimly aware of Dani flinging her arms around her new husband—of sighs from the assembled guests and of the fact she was growing colder and colder.

Somehow she managed to smile, to endure the endless photographs, to say what needed to be said—*congratulations, so pleased, yes, she looks beautiful, very happy together*—all the while aware of Cristiano taking charge and making sure his sister enjoyed every moment of her special day, his own pain ruthlessly subdued by his awesome willpower.

He was capable of caring, she thought miserably. But sometimes he got it horribly, horribly wrong.

Clumsy, not cruel.

Secure in the knowledge that all attention was on the bride and groom, Laurel slowly turned her head. Seeing that Cristiano was occupied by the bridesmaids, she allowed herself a long indulgent look, knowing it would be her last. After today she wouldn't see him again.

Storing up images, she allowed her gaze to linger on those thick lashes, travel over that strong jaw and the tempting curve of that mouth. The longing was a great tearing feeling in her chest, which made no sense at all.

She had no wish to turn the clock back.

Deep down she knew that even if he had prioritised her over work on that awful day, it wouldn't have changed anything. They might have taken a different road, but they would have ended up in the place they were now.

They didn't work well together. A relationship needed more than fiery chemistry to hold it fast.

With no warning he turned his head and caught her looking.

A frown touched his brows, as if he saw something in her face that puzzled him.

Those broad shoulders squared under the exquisitely cut suit.

Trapped by that searching, questioning gaze, Laurel ceased to breathe. She watched with her heart in her mouth as he tried to read her, *saw him use that acute brain of his to draw a conclusion from the facts at his disposal.*

One of Dani's numerous little cousins, unsettled by the size of the gathering, nestled against his legs, seeking security. Cristiano responded instantly, dragging his gaze from Laurel's pinched white face and swinging the child into his arms, offering that security instinctively and without question. The little girl buried her head in his shoulder and he lifted a hand and stroked those blonde curls, his hand strong and reassuring, his lips moving as he soothed and calmed.

It was like a slap, the display of masculine protectiveness so perfectly timed that it snapped the nostalgia that had rendered her immobile. This was Cristiano at his best. With everyone around him depending on him.

It was ironic, she thought, that the one time she'd allowed herself to do that he hadn't been there for her.

Feeling control slide from her grip, Laurel slid discreetly out of the group and forged her way through the guests to the other end of the terrace. If she took the long way round she could make it back to the villa unseen. This was her opportunity to make her final exit from his life with the minimum of fuss. She'd pack now and make her way to the airport. Forget waiting until the morning. She was willing to take a flight anywhere, as long as it meant getting out of Sicily tonight.

'What's going on, Laurel?'

Santo stood in front of her and the fact that it should be him who witnessed her distress was all the more humiliating.

'I need to be on my own.'

Strong fingers caught her chin and lifted her face, the frown descending like black clouds as he saw her eyes. 'You're crying. Now why would you be crying, I wonder?'

'I've been staring into the sun.'

'Why are you leaving?'

Desperate, she threw everything she had. 'Because it was crazy to come here. A divorce and a wedding don't go together.'

'I was watching your face. When Dani said her vows, you looked as if someone was removing your skin with a knife.'

The image made her wince because it was exactly how she'd felt. 'The death of a marriage is always sad.'

'I wasn't looking at a woman grieving for the death of her marriage.'

Oh, God, why now? Why couldn't he just leave her alone? 'You saw me upset. Was it hard for me to witness two people exchange those vows? Yes, it was hard. It doesn't change the fact that Cristiano and I are finished.'

'Why? You're obviously still in love with him.'

'I'm *not* in love with him!' Her foot almost slipped on the step. 'It's…you're…I'm just *not*.' She didn't want to be. She *couldn't* be. That would be like almost drowning in the sea and then telling someone you loved water.

'I have never seen a woman work so hard not to look at a man as you tried not to look at Cristiano during the wedding. Were you afraid that if you looked at him, he'd see what you felt? You always had this thing, didn't you—' he spread his hands in an expressive Mediterranean gesture '—this thing where you could read each other's minds. You each knew what the other was thinking. He used to tease me about it—used to tell me that one day I'd find a woman I connected with, the way he connected with you.'

Laurel felt as if she was about to connect with the ground. Any moment now she was going to faint and smack her head on the concrete. 'Worry about your own love life, Santo, and leave me to worry about mine.' She tried to pass him but he caught her arm in a firm grip.

'What you did almost destroyed my brother. I

had to watch him drag himself through every day. Losing you was like losing the oxygen from the air. Without you, he couldn't breathe.'

Laurel couldn't breathe either. Her chest was tight and her lungs were burning. 'Santo—'

'The funny thing is, I didn't believe in love until I saw the two of you together.'

Laurel ducked quickly under his arm and started to run.

She had minutes, she guessed. Minutes in which to pack her things and get safely away from the villa before he came after her.

Minutes to end this thing for good.

The sky had turned from fiery red to a rich velvet black, embedded with stars. If there was ever a moment to believe in romance and happy endings it was now but Laurel was a non-believer.

It was over, and she needed to get out of here.

CHAPTER FIVE

FROM the far end of the terrace, Cristiano watched the exchange between his wife and his brother. The child in his arms said something to him and he answered automatically before lowering her to the ground and encouraging her to play with her friends. His mind was wrapped up in Laurel.

During the wedding he'd been determined to ignore her. Not to allow his own private hell to intrude on his sister's special day. It was only when Santo had nudged him that he'd caught the expression on her face and known instantly that her mind was in the same place as his. He'd seen the betraying glisten of moisture on her cheeks and it had stunned him because in all the time they'd been together, at no time during their intense, crazy love affair had he ever seen her shed a tear. She was the toughest, strongest woman he'd ever met.

'Go after her.' Santo was by his side, smooth and in control, somehow managing to be the perfect host while talking to his brother in a low voice. 'Go now, because she'll be out of here in minutes.'

'She's complicated.'

'All women are complicated. I don't pretend to understand any of them but I do know one thing—' Santo scooped a glass of champagne from a passing waitress '—if there is such a thing as love, then that woman loves you. Move. I'll cover for you.'

Cristiano stood in frozen silence, remembering the look on her face during the photographs.

Longing. And intense sadness, as if the situation was sucking her down and drowning her.

And that didn't make sense.

Why would she be sad if this was what she wanted? If she no longer had feelings for him, why did she find all this so stressful?

It came to him in a single blinding flash of comprehension and he pressed his fingers to his forehead, his hand unsteady, the shock of it rocking his composure.

No matter how vehement her denials, it was obvious now that she *did* love him. It was also obvious that loving him was scaring her to death. She was running because she was afraid of giving in to those feelings. She didn't want to forgive him because she was afraid to forgive him. *Afraid to trust him again.*

Behind him he heard the music start, whoops of laughter and knew that soon there'd be dancing.

Propelled by an anger directed towards himself as well as her, Cristiano strode into the villa with the subtlety of the police carrying out an armed raid. The door crashed shut behind him and Laurel flew from the bedroom, eyes wide.

'What's happened?'

Just in time, Cristiano thought grimly, noticing the small suitcase lying at the foot of the enormous bed. Santo had been right. A few minutes later and she would have been gone.

Driven by a burning determination to unveil the truth, he didn't pause in his stride. Instead he just walked right up to her and backed her into the wall, planting his arms either side of her so that she was caged and completely at his mercy.

Now try and run. Now try and get out of that, my beauty.

The intensity of the rage building inside him was shocking and she must have seen something in his face because her eyes widened.

'What the hell is *wrong* with you?'

She squirmed against him but he pressed her back, using just enough of his superior strength to stop her running. She was like an animal caught in a trap, twisting and panting as she struggled to free herself, sobbing with frustration when his only response was to hold her tighter.

'You're not going anywhere.' He fisted his hand into her hair, feeling the dark mass dislodge itself and tumble over his wrist. *So silky, so soft.* 'You're not leaving this room until you've admitted how you feel.'

'Right now? Tired of being around you.'

'You're lying. You want this as much as I do—' He brought his mouth down to hers because he couldn't help himself, all the anger, the desperation, the raw emotion transmitting itself in that one physical act. He kissed her as if he'd never touched her before and never would again, as if she was the air he had to breathe to stay alive, the blood that kept his heart pumping. Her mouth was warm and sweet, the taste of her going straight to his head and pouring through his senses. Like a dangerous drug, she seeped through him, turning anger to another equally potent emotion.

He was dimly aware that she'd stopped thumping him and was now clutching him, her slim fingers locked in his shirt as her mouth opened under the pressure of his. Heat ripped through the two of them, searing the last of his control, and he scooped her up without thought or hesitation and carried her the few strides to the enormous bed that overlooked the private pool and, beyond that, the gentle curve of the beach. It was possibly the most idyllic setting on earth but neither saw it. Their focus was on each other as they devoured each other.

His trousers hit the floor, swiftly followed by her silk dress, and then he rolled her onto her back, her loosened hair melting over the silk sheets like dark chocolate pouring over whipped cream. A thin strip of lace was all that protected her from him and he ripped it away, exposing her, dizzy with his need for her. This time she was hiding nothing, he vowed. *Not one single part of herself.* He covered her with his body, prepared to use his weight to keep her still but her arms were round his neck and she met him halfway, her mouth lifting to his as his head descended. Like a starving man he feasted and she did the same, making little noises in her throat as she sank her fingers into his hair and demanded as much as she gave. His tongue was in her mouth, one hand cupping the softness of her cheek while the other found the tempting curve of her breast.

Details blurred as they tasted, touched and teased. It was wild, bordering on violent and at one point he wasn't sure if she was fighting him or urging him on as they rolled in a tangle of limbs and slick flesh, animalistic in their need for each other. He sank his teeth into her shoulder and she scraped her nails down his back, her sob turning to a gasp as he moved his hand between her legs. His fingers slid into her slick softness and he felt her writhe with the pleasure, that creamy, taut body shifting restlessly against the sheets as she tried to relieve the nagging ache in her pelvis. He touched her the way he knew she needed to be touched and her response confirmed everything he'd suspected. *She was as crazy about him as he was about her.* Here, in the most intimate situation of all, she couldn't hide from him.

And he couldn't hide from the truth.

He didn't want a divorce.

He wanted his wife. Here. Now.

Forever.

With a low growl Cristiano moved down her body and used his mouth on her, demanding every last secret from this woman who had haunted every part of his life since he'd met her. He licked in tiny tortuous circles, feeling her velvety softness tighten around his fingers, hearing her sob his name as she shattered into a million pieces.

Temptation, sensation—he considered himself a controlled man but there was no control in this room, not with her naked beneath him. Merciless and unrelenting, he sent her rushing towards her peak again and again until finally she sobbed his name and he levered himself over her and entered her with a smooth purposeful thrust of pure possession that brought a groan to the back of his throat.

She was his, and she'd always been his.

The searing heat was incredible.

His eyes closed.

As her body tightened around his he felt his mind blank and his heart split. It had always been like this between them. So much more than just sex. A joining that was far beyond the physical. No matter what had been wrong, this had always made it right. Oblivious to everything except the moment, he surged into her, each hard, deliberate stroke driving them higher. He made her his in every possible way, drawing every last drop of response from her until she was sobbing with the sheer overload of physical pleasure. The explosion was a culmination of two years of deprivation and denial. Like a deadly storm it came crashing down on them, a destructive force shattering their differences and drowning them in agonizing pleasure. Again and again it rolled over them and his mouth was on hers as his body experienced something close to sexual meltdown.

Dimly aware that she was crying, he tried to haul himself out of the grip of passion but he was weakened by the shocking impact of what they'd shared, powerless to stop the tears pouring down her cheeks as she sobbed something incoherent against his mouth.

Trying to understand what she was saying, he dragged his mouth from hers and just about made out his name and then the words, '*I can't do this again—*'

The emotion caught him full in the chest and he felt his own throat close. With a rough curse he held her tightly, crushing her against him in a possessive gesture as they both slowly recovered.

She trembled and sobbed against him until his

chest was damp, strands of her hair caught between the two of them. Two years ago he would have been appalled if someone had told him he'd be pleased to see her crying. But in a savage, primitive way he *was* pleased. In fact he was close to exultant because Laurel so rarely showed her emotions. For her to do so now was an indication of what she was feeling and he knew that if there was ever a time to persuade her to talk to him then it was now, while she was weakened and vulnerable.

Cruel? Maybe. She'd already accused him of that, hadn't she?

He'd never been one to back down when there was something that needed doing.

Stroking her damp hair out of her eyes, he dried her tears, ruthlessly closing down that side of him that retreated from the prospect of upsetting her further. She breathed with a hitch and a judder, everything uneven, but there was no sign of an impending asthma attack. Which was a relief because nothing, not volcanic eruption or earthquake, nor the sharp sting of his conscience was going to interrupt *this* conversation.

Her eyes were reddened and swollen, her mouth bruised from his kisses. *His* kisses.

His resolve turned to steel and he stared down at her, knowing that he couldn't allow her time to put those barriers up again. He was still inside her. *Still hard*, he realised as he ruefully acknowledged the effect she had on him.

It didn't get any more intimate than this, he thought grimly, and he wanted intimate.

He wanted it all.

Everything they'd lost, and more.

Holding her still, trapping her with his strength, he took her chin in his hand and turned her tear-streaked face to his. '*Now* tell me you're not in love with me.'

Laurel lay in shock, wrung out from the deluge of emotion and the mind-blowing sex. Emotionally and physically spent, she just wanted to roll over and bury her head in the pillow but he lay in a position of domination, the muscles of his sleek, powerful shoulders bunched as he protected her from his weight, waiting for her response to his all male command. She tried to pull herself back, to separate herself, but they were entwined in every way possible. She could still feel him, hard and heavy, and her body tensed around him, drawing a soft curse from his lips.

'Don't move—'

'*You* move then—'

'I'm not going anywhere until you admit the way you feel—' His voice was a thickened growl and she knew him well enough to know that he wasn't going to back off until she'd spoken the words he wanted to hear.

And she had no intention of doing that. 'You're heavy. I can't breathe properly.'

The connection was sweet and terrifying at the same time and her hips moved without her consent, the unconsciously sensuous movement dragging another curse from his lips.

Drawing in a long breath, he closed one strong hand over her hip, holding her still while he struggled for control. 'I said *don't* move.'

'I need fresh air.'

'Coward.'

Was she a coward? No, she wasn't. She was strong. She'd survived an upbringing that would have wrecked many people but the grim, cold reality of her early life had taught her one important lesson: that life was about choices. And she'd been fiercely determined to make the best choices she could.

So what was she doing back in Cristiano's bed?

Bad choice, she thought desperately, but then remembered that the length of time he'd allowed her to make that choice could have been measured in milliseconds.

'You're a very attractive guy, Cristiano, no woman is likely to dispute that. So we just had sex.'

'I noticed.' His mouth curved into a satisfied masculine smile and he shifted his body just enough to make her gasp. 'So what does that make you?'

'Stupid.'

Despite the fact she wasn't saying the words he wanted to hear, he was still smiling, but this time there were hints of the sardonic about the curve of his mouth. 'You're not stupid, but you *are* a liar, *tesoro*. And you *are* in love with me.'

'You're *so* arrogant. The world does not begin and end with you.'

'It does to you. Admit it.' He held her trapped and she squirmed beneath him and then stilled as she felt him grow harder.

'Get *off* me or I'm going to have to hurt you.'

'You're strong, but I'm stronger.' He spoke through his teeth, clearly as affected by their physical connection as she was. 'Tell me why you walked out on us. Why didn't you just yell at me and fix it?'

'Because I didn't want to fix it.' She wasn't used to feeling helpless and he made her feel helpless. 'You're a selfish bastard and I don't want to spend the rest of my life with you. We're not good together.'

'No, you're right. We're terrible together.' His mouth was right up against hers, his words blending with her lips, his breath warm and seductive. 'I may be a selfish bastard but I love you.'

Her heart melted. He always did this. He always

knew exactly what to say to thrust her off balance. 'You'll get over it.'

Choices, she reminded herself. *It was all about choices.*

His low laugh was accompanied by the slow, sneaky brush of his mouth against hers. 'Just for the record, how many men do you scream underneath in an average week?'

'You're disgusting.'

'I'm honest. And maybe a touch possessive,' he conceded, 'but I have no problems with you being the same. I happen to believe what we have is worth fighting hard to protect, otherwise I wouldn't be here.' Strong fingers caught her chin and the humour died in his eyes. 'Say it. Say *I love you.*'

'Because we just had sex? Your superior technique was supposed to have the same effect as a mind wipe? It was a physical act, Cristiano. It had no emotional meaning.'

He swore under his breath and finally shifted his weight. Rolling onto his back, he jabbed his fingers into his hair in a gesture of frustration. 'You drive me insane, you know that, don't you?'

'Likewise.' She'd wanted him to let her go, but now that he had she felt the loss of it keenly.

That was the way they'd always slept, she remembered, holding onto each other. She'd never depended on anyone, ever, but the way she'd slept with Cristiano had been the nearest she'd come to relaxing that rule.

It had made night her favourite time.

She felt herself weaken.

She was about to turn to him when he rose from the bed, gloriously indifferent to the fact he was naked. He was completely comfortable with himself. His ego had been nurtured by an adoring family and fattened by the admiration of all who came into contact with him. He was the golden boy. The Prince.

The muscles of his torso rippled as he moved and she felt her instant response, although how she could even contemplate more sex after what they'd just shared she had no idea.

Even so, everything inside her softened and melted and when he turned his dark, proud head to look at her she felt the same connection that had drawn them together the first time they'd met.

'Why do women always turn everything into a major drama?' His exasperated question was so unexpected that Laurel froze.

'Sorry?'

'So I made a mistake—' He spread his hands in what she assumed was intended as a gesture of apology. 'I should have been there, but I wasn't. Why does this have to become an insurmountable barrier between us? Yes, it was unfortunate, but you would throw everything away because of one day when I made a bad decision?'

Unfortunate?

The blurring in her brain cleared. Everything that had softened, hardened again. 'At least you're agreeing you made a bad decision,' she said shakily. 'I suppose that's a start.'

He eyed her with extreme caution, as if she were a bomb he didn't quite know how to defuse. 'If I'd known how upset you were going to be, then *obviously* I would have chosen differently, but the negotiations on the Caribbean deal were at an extremely delicate stage.'

Delicate? Laurel thought of herself, alone in the hospital bed, being told the news. He had no idea, she thought numbly. No idea what she'd been through and she hadn't even bothered telling him because it had been irrelevant. 'So you're saying that it was only a bad decision because of my reaction. If I'd been a tolerant Sicilian wife then prioritising your work over everything else would have been acceptable.'

'That hotel has been our most successful. Had I not shown up that day we would have lost the bid.'

'So what you're actually saying is that the business was more important than me and you don't actually regret it because it's making you a nice profit.'

'Once again you are twisting everything I say!'

'Nothing is twisted. Everything is straight in my head.'

'It is done, now. Finished. I don't see the point in looking back.'

'Well, it's nice to know you're not beating yourself up over it,' Laurel said stiffly. 'I'd hate to think your guilty conscience was keeping you awake at night.'

His eyes glinted. 'I'm just saying that it is a useless waste of energy to dwell on the past. It can never be changed.'

'True, but it can be used as a useful indicator of how to behave in the future. It's called learning from mistakes. Something you're not so good at, presumably because your ego blocks the view.' Galvanised into action by his total lack of self-awareness, Laurel jumped out of bed and stumbled over to her suitcase, which lay abandoned on the floor.

Shocked and horrified by how close she'd come to allowing herself to be seduced right back to where they'd come from, she yanked at the zip, aware that he was watching her with incredulity.

'What the hell are you doing now?'

'Getting out of here. It's what I was trying to do before you barged through that door and used sex as a weapon.'

'I did *not* use sex as a weapon.' His jaw hardened and his eyes turned a dangerous shade of black. 'Unless you count using it to try and crack that tough outer shell of yours.'

'I have that tough outer shell to protect myself from people like you.'

'I loved you. I still love you.' His voice thickened as he exposed his soul. 'I made the ultimate commitment, but apparently that meant nothing to you. And still means nothing to you.'

'You never loved me, Cristiano. You loved the challenge, the chase—' She flung open the case. 'Maybe you loved the fact I was the only woman who didn't stare when you walked past, that I wasn't impressed by the money and the status. I don't know—but I *do* know it wasn't love. The only thing you love is your work. That comes first for you. Nothing turns you on like winning a deal.'

His jaw was rigid. 'I loved you. But you were afraid of that. Your problem is that you can't let yourself need someone.'

'And that drives you mad, doesn't it? You can't have a relationship with someone who doesn't need you. You don't want an equal, you want a dependent because it makes you feel big and macho.' They were fighting and both of them knew that the reason the emotion was so agonisingly raw was because they cared so much. 'You *made* me need you. You pushed and you pushed until you made holes in the armour I've spent all my life creating and then you walked off and left me exposed and I hate you for that.' She tugged a T-shirt out of the case.

'Then why didn't you tell me instead of just walking out? That was cowardly.'

'It was survival.'

'I arrived home after that trip, ready to offer you support and you sat there in silence. You said virtually nothing except, "I'm leaving you."'

She'd had no words to communicate what she'd been feeling. She'd been swallowed up by emotions so huge and terrifying that she'd barely been able to function.

'There was nothing to say.' Laurel was pulling on her clothes. Not the silky bridesmaid dress that still lay abandoned where he'd dropped it so carelessly, but the skinny jeans she'd jammed into her suitcase moments before he'd crashed his way into the room. 'This conversation is over. My flight leaves in an hour.'

'Then they're leaving with one less passenger.' His rough, raw tone would have stopped a lesser woman in her tracks but Laurel jammed her feet into her shoes.

'I'm going to be on that flight and if you dare try and stop me I'll call the police.' She ignored the fact that the Chief of Police regularly dined with the Ferraras. 'The divorce is already going ahead. I saw Carlo this morning and signed everything you wanted me to sign.'

'That's irrelevant now.'

'What do you mean, irrelevant?' She zipped her jeans and freed the long sweep of her hair from the neck of her scarlet shirt. His eyes followed the movement and she tried not to remember how many times he'd buried his fingers in her hair as he'd kissed her.

'Italian law expressly declares that a separation must be physical to be valid. A couple has to be formally separated for three years before a decree can be issued.' His eyes slid from her hair to her mouth, his intimate and deliberate gaze reminding her of what they'd just done.

As the meaning behind his statement slowly sank in she felt a sick feeling in the pit of her stomach. Had she inadvertently sent the clock back to the beginning? No. *Not that.* 'You can't be serious.'

'Even if we hadn't just proved that we can't be apart for that length of time, there is no way I'd be giving you a divorce now.' His voice was like steel and she was suddenly aware of her heart hammering against her chest.

'There's no one you can't influence. You could arrange it if you wanted to.'

'I *don't* want to.'

'Yes, you do! You hate me for leaving you.' Desperately she tried to stoke his anger but he was maddeningly cool.

'And you hate me for going into one more meeting when I should have flown home to be with you. We both made mistakes. Being married is about fixing them and moving forwards. That's what we're doing.'

He was so smug, she thought desperately as she zipped the suitcase shut and grabbed the handle. So arrogantly sure that all he had to do was snap his fingers and whatever he wanted to happen would happen. So confident that he could wipe away the past.

'You think we can move forward, but you have no idea what happened on that day.' She was shaking with the stress of thinking about it. 'You don't know how I felt.'

His icy exterior splintered. 'So *tell* me how you felt. Tell me now. Don't hold anything back.'

The suitcase landed on the floor with a dull thump. 'It started with a pain, low in my stomach.' Her voice was remarkably steady given the fact that this was the conversation she'd thought she'd never have. 'I thought to myself, *This isn't right*. I called you, but your PA told me that you couldn't be disturbed.'

His jaw tightened, like a fighter bracing himself for a punch. Clearly these weren't the feelings he wanted to hear. 'Laurel—'

'I don't hold that against you.' She didn't give him time to speak. It was her turn now and she intended to use it. 'The first message didn't get through but that was her fault, not yours. And my fault for not being more forceful about needing to speak to you. I called the doctor and he told me to take painkillers and go back to bed and rest for a while, so I did that and the pain grew worse. I knew no one else in Sicily. Your mother was staying with her sister in Rome, Santo was with you in the Caribbean. I was alone. And frightened.' Her emphasis on that word triggered an indefinable change in him. 'I called you again. This time I was forceful. I insisted on speaking to you and she put me through—' Her heart rate doubled and she was back in that room; back with the pain and the panic. She remembered again the terrifying sense of isolation. 'You asked me if I was bleeding and when I said I wasn't you spoke to the doctor and between you, you decided that I was a neurotic woman.'

'That is *not* true. At no point did I accuse you of neuroses.' He sprang to his own defence but Laurel wasn't in the mood to listen.

'You were always labouring the fact that I found it hard to tell you how I was feeling. *"Trust me,"* you said in that same seductive voice you always use when you're determined to get your own way. So I did. On that day, I put all my trust in you. I told you I thought something was badly wrong and that I didn't trust the doctor. I told you I was scared. That's the first and only time I've admitted that to anyone. For the first time in our relationship I put my trust in you and your response to that enormous risk on my part was to dismiss my concerns as less valid than the doctor's and return to your meeting. With your phone switched off.'

She saw the exact moment he recognised the impact of that decision.

His breathing turned shallow. His bronzed handsome face lost some of its colour. 'It was a particularly bad moment—'

'It was a particularly bad moment for me, too.' This time she wasn't letting him off the hook. 'When you said, *"I have to go now, but I'll call you later. Don't worry, you'll be fine,"* how did you think I'd feel?'

'I was trying to reassure you.'

'No, you were trying to reassure yourself. You needed to convince yourself I'd be fine in order to justify staying there and not immediately flying home. You made the judgement that I was overreacting. You didn't once think about the fact I had never asked you for anything before. You didn't think of me at all, so don't talk to me about love. Even if I hadn't lost the baby, the fact that I'd asked for your help when I'd never, ever called you at work before should have been enough.' The words poured out of her along with her feelings and there was nothing she could do to stop it now because her control had been swept away by the violent force of her emotions. 'You say that I killed our marriage by walking out but it was your empty, useless verbal pat on the head that did that. It was the first time in my life I'd asked another human being for help. And you dismissed me. And because I was panicking, because I couldn't actually believe that you'd done that, I phoned you one more time, only to discover that you'd turned your phone off.'

He stood immobile, as if every shot she'd fired had gone straight into his brain. 'You didn't tell me that you felt that way.'

'Well, I'm telling you now. And do you know the worst thing?' It had been hard to open up but now that she had, the hard part was stopping. 'Because I had allowed myself to trust you, depend on you, for one horrible minute I actually thought that I couldn't handle the situation without your help. I actually had to remind myself that before you came along and insisted on being the macho protector, I did perfectly well by myself. Once I'd reminded myself of that fact, I calmed down and took myself to hospital.' She emphasized the word 'myself' but it was the word 'hospital' that drew his attention and had his brows meeting in a deep frown.

'You went to the hospital? Why was that necessary?'

'Because neither my doctor nor my husband believed anything was wrong. Fortunately I knew differently.' She watched the tension spread across those wide, powerful shoulders. Standing there naked, he should have looked vulnerable but Cristiano didn't know how to look vulnerable. Even in this most sensitive of situations, he was the one in command.

'I had no idea you went to hospital. You should have told me.'

'When? When was I supposed to tell you? I *tried* telling you but you had switched your phone off to avoid the inconvenience of talking to your neurotic wife. By the time you finally fitted me into your demanding schedule, I'd coped with it by myself. There was no point in telling you.'

'Now you're being childish.'

The accusation robbed her of breath. 'I asked for your help, you didn't give it. I told you I was scared, you didn't come. Did you really think I was going to carry on begging for attention? I did what I've always done. I sorted it. That isn't childish, Cristiano. It's adult behaviour.'

'Adults don't walk away from a difficult situation.' A muscle flickered in his jaw. 'Even given the difficult circumstances, there was no excuse for sulking.'

'Sulking?' Her voice shook and she could barely say the words that needed to be said. To steady herself, she took a slow, deep breath. 'God, you have no idea. I don't know why I'm even wasting my breath having this conversation. You say I don't talk but the biggest problem is that you don't listen. I say, "I'm in trouble" and you hear, *She's neurotic; she'll be fine*. If that's love, then I don't want it or need it.' Dragging her phone from her bag, Laurel punched in a number and ordered a taxi in shaky Italian, shocked by the powerful and utterly alien urge to leap on him and do him physical harm.

Watching her through eyes glittering with frustration, Cristiano dragged in a driven breath. 'You will not leave this room until we've finished talking.'

'Watch me.'

'*Basta!* Enough!' His face as pale as Sicilian marble, his muscular frame taut, he blocked her path. 'I realise that a miscarriage is a shattering experience for a woman. I, too, was very upset at the loss of the pregnancy, but it's important to keep this in perspective. These things happen. My mother lost two babies and then went on to have three healthy pregnancies. Our problem is not the miscarriage, it is our marriage. If we can sort that out then we will have more children.'

Laurel stood still, frozen by the chill of her own emotions, wondering how someone so emotionally expressive could be so monumentally insensitive towards the feelings of others. 'We won't be having more children, Cristiano.'

'I made you pregnant the first time we had unprotected sex. After tonight you could already be pregnant. You probably are.' His unquestioning confidence in his own virility increased her tension tenfold.

'I'm not pregnant.' Her lips were stiff and the blood pounded through her skull. 'That isn't possible.'

'A miscarriage doesn't—'

'I didn't have a miscarriage.'

His brows met in a frown. 'But—'

'I had an ectopic pregnancy.' Just saying it brought back the memories and she had to pause and hitch in her breath, which surprised her because she'd thought that by now the experience should have been nothing more than a bad memory. She pressed the flat of her hand to her abdomen, to that part of her that had malfunctioned with such devastating consequences. *She thought of their child.* 'If I hadn't followed my instinct and gone to hospital when I did, there is a strong chance I would have died when the tube ruptured. As it was, they operated within fifteen minutes of my arrival and they saved my life. I owe them that. They were brilliant.'

The silence was shattering.

She'd never witnessed Cristiano at a loss. She'd never witnessed him unsure and out of his depth.

But she was witnessing it now.

The blistering self-belief was nowhere in evidence and he actually shifted his position as if he needed to rebalance himself, the foundations of his rock-solid confidence severely shaken by her unexpected admission.

Deciding that it was only fair to give him the right of response, Laurel waited.

And waited.

No sound emerged from his lips. His face was the colour of pale marble and his hands were clenched into fists by his sides. He looked utterly shattered by her dramatic revelation.

'You should have told me.' His hoarse exhortation shattered the silence. 'It was wrong of you not to.'

Any sympathy she might have felt dissolved in that unguarded, judgemental comment. Even now, it seemed, the fault was hers.

'If you'd been here, I wouldn't have had to tell you,' she snapped, her hand closing round the handle of her suitcase. 'The doctor would have told you. And he also would have told you that I can't have more children. They removed one tube and the other is such a mess there is no way it's up to the job, so you'll have to find someone else on whom to publicly demonstrate your astonishing virility.' Eyes stinging, throat dry, she hauled the suitcase towards the door, knowing that the taxi would already be waiting. If there was one thing you could depend on in a Ferrara hotel, it was efficiency and attentiveness to the needs of the guests. It was just a shame that same attentiveness hadn't spilled over into their marriage. 'Don't follow me, Cristiano. I don't have anything left to say to you.'

CHAPTER SIX

THE door slammed.

Cristiano flinched, the sound reverberating through his skull.

He stared at the empty space that moments before had held Laurel and her suitcase. *A furious, fire-breathing Laurel.* Even when he heard the revving sound of an engine vanishing into the distance he still didn't move. He was incapable of moving. His brain and body felt disconnected, frozen at the point she'd made her shocking confession.

Ectopic pregnancy?

She'd almost died?

As the stark, shocking truth sank into his brain he stumbled through to the bathroom and was violently ill.

His brain produced a kaleidoscope of vile images. Laurel clutching her phone, confessing that she had a bad feeling. Him, switching his phone off while he went into one more meeting. And the worst image of all—a bunch of gowned surgeons battling to save the life of the woman he loved.

A life he hadn't even known was at risk.

A love she didn't believe in.

Trying to clear his head, Cristiano lurched into the shower and turned the jets on full force and the temperature to cold.

Minutes later he was shivering, but his brain still wasn't functioning.

He kept thinking of her alone in a hospital room, her fears dismissed by those closest to her.

Her accusation that he was the one who had pushed her to confide in him and trust him rang loud in his brain. He remembered that single phone call with uncomfortable clarity, including the part where he'd placed all his trust in the doctor's opinion and dismissed her anxieties.

Phone call. He had to make a phone call.

Cristiano turned off the shower, knotted a towel around his hips and sleepwalked back into the bedroom, trying to remember where he'd put his phone. He stared blankly at his suit, strewn carelessly on the floor in the hot burn of passion.

She'd almost died.

Picking up his trousers, he fumbled blindly in the pockets. No phone. Surely he'd had it with him last night?

Why hadn't the hospital called him when she was admitted?

Distracted by that question, he picked up his jacket and his phone slid out of the pocket and fell onto the tiled floor with an ominous crack.

Broken, he thought. Like everything else around him. And all through his own carelessness.

Trying not to compare that livid line now dividing the screen with the state of his marriage, Cristiano punched in the number of the hospital, relieved to find that the phone still worked.

His reputation meant that he was instantly put through to the relevant person.

Unsettled to find that the hand holding the phone was shaking, he sank onto the sofa.

When the consultant at the hospital refused to divulge any information on Laurel's case without her permission, Cristiano tried asserting his authority but in truth he had none and the man wouldn't betray patient confidentiality.

Feeling uncomfortably as if he was losing his grip, Cristiano pulled on his clothes from the night before and dropped his shattered phone into the pocket of his trousers.

Nothing the doctor told him would have changed the way he was feeling anyway.

The details about what had happened at the hospital were irrelevant now. Wasn't he the one who always said that you had to keep moving forward? And here he was, rooted to the spot, beating himself up about the past while she was currently boarding a plane, intent on getting as far away from him as possible.

He had to stop her.

Still in the process of buttoning his shirt, Cristiano grabbed his car keys and sprinted from the villa, leaving the door wide open. He sprang into his sports car and accelerated away, exploiting his skill and knowledge to push the car to the limits of its capability. Dust rose behind him, smothering his stunned security team in a choking white cloud.

Part of him was aware that he was behaving like a madman but he didn't even care.

She did this to him, he thought, finally finding focus as he shifted gears. She drove him to behave in ways he had never behaved before. Take marriage—he braked sharply and swerved to avoid an oncoming car—he'd been perfectly happy with his single status until he'd met Laurel.

Santo had employed her to train him for the New York City Marathon and had suggested she advise on the hotel development.

Right from the first moment he'd seen her, Cristiano had been lost.

She'd walked into his office, that chocolate-brown ponytail swinging, and calmly pointed out all the flaws in the plans for the new state-of-the-art fitness centre.

Other people tiptoed around him, intimidated by

the power he wielded. Most of them were too protective of their own futures to challenge him.

Laurel had shown no such reservations. She had absolute faith in her own expertise, a confidence that came from a lifetime of making decisions alone. He'd learned quickly that the only person she trusted in life was herself.

In his head he heard her voice on that day she'd come to his office to give him her recommendations.

'You hired me,' she'd reminded him in a cool voice as she'd scored lines through the list of equipment and added more. 'I presume you want my professional opinion. Your entire model is flawed. No one wants to come to a hotel of this quality and sweat on a treadmill. You need personal trainers. One to one. Everything tailored to the individual. You need free weights, exercise balls, offer Pilates—' Her list had been carefully thought out. It had been her idea to turn what had originally been a standard gym into an exclusive fitness club, including physiotherapy and links to the spa with massage and beauty treatments. 'You'll attract athletes, but also normal people because you're developing tailored programmes. In an ideal world everyone should have a personal programme and you're trying to create an ideal world.'

When he'd pointed out the cost of her plans, she'd laughed. 'Do you want to be the best or not?'

Despite grumblings from his brother, he'd followed her proposal to the last detail, admiring her bold vision and her innate sense of what was possible.

It had been an overwhelming success.

The Ferrara Spa Resort was now one of Europe's foremost hotels. They did indeed attract top athletes who were able to maintain fitness within the luxurious resort, but they also drew a less physically fit clientele eager to make use of the expertise on offer. Laurel had personally selected the staff, trained them and supervised those opening weeks to ensure that everything was the very best it could be. She worked like a Trojan.

Cristiano had offered her a small fortune to stay on and run it but she'd turned him down flat.

'I don't work for other people.' She was the most independent, self-reliant woman he'd ever met. Ironic, he mused, that the very quality that had drawn him had been the one that had eventually torn them apart.

Because of him. *Because of his blind, selfish behaviour.*

There had been reasons, of course. Reasons for switching off his phone and trying to block out all distractions. Reasons for choosing to stay instead of fly home. But he hadn't shared those reasons because any explanation he delivered now would be seen as an excuse. And there was no excuse for the arrogant, thoughtless way he'd dismissed her fears.

No pile of bricks, no piece of land was worth the price they'd both paid.

Cristiano released the brakes and fed in the throttle, reaching the airport in record time.

Violating at least three traffic laws, he abandoned the car at the front of the terminal building and strode through the glass doors to Departures.

This part of the airport was unfamiliar to him and it was like walking into hell, a teeming mass of bad-tempered humanity crushed together into a woefully inadequate space.

Tripping over an ill-placed suitcase, Cristiano regained his balance and looked round, desperately trying to spot Laurel in the crowd. It seemed an impossible task. The place was heaving with tourists trying to move enormous suitcases through an unyielding, irritated throng. Faces glowed scarlet from too much Sicilian sun and too little cream, babies screamed, toddlers were fractious with boredom, mothers harassed, fathers bad tempered.

It was a place Cristiano had never had reason to visit before and looking at it now he had no regrets about that. *Why did people come on holiday?* he thought as he took advantage of his superior height to see over the heads of a group of scantily clad, giggling teenage girls.

He was just about to locate someone in authority

and demand that they make an announcement over the public address system when he spotted a shiny brown ponytail towards the front of the check-in desk for Heathrow.

Laurel.

Hot and sticky, Laurel handed her ticket to the woman on the desk.

'I'd like an aisle seat if possible, please.'

She didn't want to look out of the window. She wanted to read a book and shut Sicily out of her mind.

A different woman would have sobbed all the way to the airport, but Laurel was in full crisis mode, focusing on getting out of Sicily and back to London as fast as possible.

She felt numb, slightly removed from everything that was happening around her.

Because of that, she wasn't aware of the commotion behind her until she noticed a group of women in an adjoining queue all staring in awe.

Laurel recognised that look.

She'd seen it a million times on the faces of women when they caught sight of Cristiano.

Heart thumping, she turned her head to follow the direction of their stares and saw him forging his way through throngs of gawping tourists. Her first reaction was one of astonishment. She knew for certain he'd never been into this part of the airport before and he looked ridiculously out of place, like a thoroughbred horse in a field of donkeys.

Astonishment changed to alarm as it dawned on her that there was only one explanation for him being here. He wanted to stop her leaving.

And she didn't want to be stopped.

She didn't want to listen to anything he had to say.

As he vaulted smoothly over a pile of suitcases blocking his path, she backed away from him.

'Go away. I have *nothing* left to say to you.'

'You may have nothing left to say to me but I have plenty to say to you.'

'My flight is boarding. I don't have time to listen.'

His eyes glowed dark and dangerous. 'If I board that plane I'll have it grounded.'

Unlike the women hovering close to her, Laurel was unimpressed. 'Then I'll board a different plane. There is nothing you can say that I want to hear.'

'You don't know that until you've listened.' He appeared oblivious to the growing audience of tourists who, sensing drama, pressed in closer.

'You want to defend yourself. It's what you always do.'

He sucked in a deep breath. For a moment she thought he was going to stretch out a hand to her but then he changed his mind and let it fall back to his side. 'Even I cannot defend the indefensible.'

A woman close to her sighed dreamily, but Laurel ignored her.

'You are finally admitting that your behaviour may have been less than perfect?'

'My behaviour was abysmal.'

It wasn't the words that caught her attention, although they were unusual enough. It was his dishevelled appearance that finally made her think that perhaps his attempts to talk were driven by conscience rather than his usual urge to prove that he was right in everything.

Before this moment she'd never seen Cristiano anything other than immaculate. But not only was he badly in need of a shave but he'd clearly left the villa halfway through the act of dragging on his clothes. 'Aren't those the trousers you wore for the wedding?'

'I was in a hurry to get here.' His bronzed face had lost layers of colour, his dark eyes shadowed with guilt. 'I grabbed the first thing I could find.'

She wondered if he even realised that half the buttons of his shirt were still undone, the result offering those gawping women a tantalising view of the most masculine chest they were likely to see in a lifetime.

'I appreciate the gesture, but it doesn't change anything. Go home, Cristiano. I don't want you.'

From somewhere behind her she heard a woman mutter, '*If she doesn't want him, I'll have him*', but

Laurel wasn't interested in anyone else's opinion on the man in question.

His eyes were feverish, the look in them close to desperation. 'Give me a chance to apologise properly.'

'Yes, give him a chance, love!' There was a chorus of encouragement from the growing crowd and one of the women grinned at her. 'If a man wants to say sorry, never stop him. It's a rare enough occurrence. Let him speak.'

All they saw was spectacular good looks and wealth and Laurel trusted neither. 'He's clever with words.'

'Lucky you. My husband can't string a sentence together that doesn't contain the words "beer" and "football".'

'Whatever he says, he won't mean it.'

'Yes, I will!' Cristiano interrupted forcefully and sent a dazzling smile towards the already starry-eyed woman. 'Thank you for your advice. I hope you've had a spectacular stay in Sicily.'

'We have, thank you very much.'

'Madam, we have your boarding card.' The girl at the check-in desk handed Laurel her passport and the card but Cristiano reached out and took it.

'We're holding up the queue. At the very least we should have this conversation somewhere else.'

'We're not having a conversation.'

'All right, I'll do it here if that's what it takes.'

'Do what?'

After the briefest hesitation, Cristiano dragged her against him and kissed her, but this kiss was nothing like the ones that had set her on fire the night before. It was a blatant attempt to dissuade her from her course and it held more than a hint of desperation.

Somewhere in the distance Laurel heard someone sigh and she resolutely ignored the flare of heat that tugged at her belly as she pulled away from him.

'That is *not* an apology.'

'I know.' His voice was a husky, apologetic groan. 'But first I had to get your attention and I don't know any other way. My brain isn't working.'

And he had her attention, just as he'd known he would. As always, he knew exactly how to turn her into a shivering, compliant mass.

'*Mi dispiace*, I'm sorry.' He murmured the words against her mouth so that even in this impersonal space, his apology was intimate and heartfelt. 'I'm sorry about our baby. I'm sorry about your frightening experience. Most of all I'm sorry that I wasn't there for you. I have so many things to say sorry for I don't know where to start.'

Tears that had been nowhere in sight when she'd stalked away from him suddenly sprang to the back of her eyes. 'It's too late.'

'*Ti amo*. I love you, Laurie.' His hands cupped her cheeks. His eyes held hers, refusing to let her look away. 'I can see why you might not believe that right now, but I *do* love you.'

'Don't say that.'

'I'll say it because it's true, although I'm the first to admit I've made a disaster of showing you. I'm clumsy and thoughtless but I love you. I love you so much I don't know how I will cope if you're not in my life and I'm too selfish to let you go.'

Thrown off balance, she rested her hands on his chest, steadying herself against the swoop of emotion that threatened to take her legs from under her. 'You'll cope perfectly. You always do.'

'That isn't true. For the past two years I have filled every hour with work to try and blot out the fact that you weren't there.'

'When I *was* here you barely saw me. Only at night.'

'Come back to me and that will change,' he vowed. '*I* will change.'

'You can't change, Cristiano. You will be in mid-conversation with me and that phone of yours will ring and suddenly I'll slide to the bottom of your list of priorities.'

'Never again,' he vowed thickly. 'From now on you're right at the top of that list and you're staying there. I've learned that lesson.'

'You're incapable of changing.'

'Give me a chance to prove you wrong.'

Never had the departure hall of the airport been

so quiet. News of the dramatic encounter at the check-in desk for the Heathrow flight appeared to have spread and now it seemed that half the passengers were listening rapt to the exchange, grateful for any distraction from the boredom and unpleasantness of the airport experience.

And now everyone was waiting for Laurel's answer.

'People don't just change overnight, Cristiano. You're *so* competitive, you're programmed to drive your business to the top. And the only reason you're here fighting for me now is because you've lost me.'

The remaining colour disappeared from his face. 'I can't lose you. I won't. I behaved appallingly, that's true, but at least give me a chance to make it up to you.'

'You can make it up to me by letting me board that flight.' She had to get out of here, she thought desperately. She had to get on that plane before she fell for his smooth patter all over again. 'Thanks for the apology. I appreciate it. And if you really are sorry then the best thing you can do is leave me to get on with the rest of my life.'

The trouble was that there *was* no smooth patter, Laurel thought numbly. This normally fluent man was stumbling like a teenager on his first date and the struggle affected her far more than any degree of polished sophistication.

Exasperated with herself for still standing here

when she should be boarding the plane, she watched as he fumbled in his pocket and drew out a slim rectangular velvet box.

'I bought you a gift.'

Laurel looked at the shape and relaxed slightly.

A diamond necklace.

This, at least, was a predictable response.

She had a diamond necklace for every row they'd ever had.

'Goodbye, Cristiano.'

'No!' He opened the box and the words froze in her mouth because nestling on a bed of blue velvet was an old rusty key.

'What on earth is that?'

'It's something I bought for you two years ago.' In the background a flight was called and his expression went from desperate to determined. 'I'd like you to see what it opens before you make up your mind that we have no future.'

It wasn't a diamond necklace.

Laurel reached out and lifted the key. It was large and surprisingly heavy. It looked as if it would open a gate of some sort, but she had no idea what gate or where it led.

Cristiano took advantage of her silence. 'You say that I was thinking of work all the time and not you, but if you come with me now I can prove that wasn't true. I understand that you can't suddenly bring yourself to trust me again, but would you at least agree to stay in Sicily for a few more weeks so that I can show you something?'

Despite her reservations, the key fascinated her and it was that, together with the growing awareness that their entangled love life was now the focus of everyone's attention that weakened her resolve. Tired of playing the starring role in a drama she hadn't scripted, Laurel looked at him. 'I'm not promising to stay for weeks. But I'll stay long enough for you to show me what this opens. Then I'll decide.'

Her words were greeted by a ripple of approval from the crowd and Laurel felt suddenly trapped. 'Don't get any ideas. This isn't forever. This is—'

'—just to get us out of this hellhole,' he muttered under his breath, flashing her a grateful smile that said he was feeling the same way as her.

He picked up her suitcase and the fascinated crowd parted in front of them. As they made it through the obstacle course of holiday luggage to the front of the building, applause broke out behind them and Cristiano rolled his eyes.

'Are they clapping you or me?'

'Probably applauding your pecs. You've had them on display for the past ten minutes.'

He glanced ruefully down at his open shirt but buttoning it up required releasing her hand or her suitcase and it appeared he was reluctant to do either. 'I have an excellent personal trainer.'

Seeing his sports car parked at an odd angle in front of the terminal building, Laurel stopped dead. 'What happened there?'

He viewed the evidence of his own dubious driving with a pained expression. 'My concentration wasn't what it might have been.'

'So it would seem.' She watched as he stowed her suitcase in the boot. The key was heavy in her hand and still she had no idea what it opened. 'Are we going back to the villa?'

The horrible feeling that she'd made the wrong decision lingered in her subconscious.

What difference was a rusty key going to make to their relationship?

Should she have held tight to the boarding card and climbed onto that plane?

'If we go back to the villa we will be mobbed by my well-meaning family. The next part of our conversation is going to be conducted without an audience.'

'So where are we going?'

'It's a surprise.'

'I'm not big on surprises.' Reminding herself that all she was giving him was the opportunity to apologise properly and without an audience, Laurel slid into the car. 'Don't you think you'd better go home first and change? Pick up some luggage?'

'No.'

'You're wearing half a tuxedo. You look ridiculous.' Except that he didn't. He looked insanely sexy, which just wasn't fair because he'd literally dragged on his clothes and still had the attention of every woman in the airport.

Including her.

The engine started with a throaty roar and he turned to look at her, his dark gaze colliding with hers. 'Do you care what I'm wearing? Does it matter?'

Even here, with horns blaring and people staring, chemistry flared hot and fierce.

She just couldn't make it die, she thought desperately, feeling the air around them grow electric and her nerve-endings start to sing. Shaken, her gaze slid to the gap in his shirt and then back to his eyes. 'Don't think sex is going to get you off the hook.'

'I don't think that.' He didn't smile. He didn't flirt. For a moment she thought he was going to say something else and then his phone rang.

The timing couldn't have been worse.

Tense as the string on a violin, she waited for him to answer it.

His hand automatically left the steering wheel to reach into his pocket and then he stopped and she saw the exact moment he made the decision not to take the call.

Laurel sighed. 'Answer it. Your empire might be crumbling.'

'Let it crumble.' Instead of returning his hand to the steering wheel, he closed it over her cold fingers. 'I know you don't think I can do this, but I can. I want to. I am going to prove to you that our marriage matters more to me than anything.'

Instead of reassuring her, his words increased her own tension levels because she knew that even if they could somehow put the past behind them, a future was impossible.

She knew it wasn't just a simple question of recreating what they'd had before.

Everything had changed.

Everything except for the dangerous chemistry that sizzled between them.

Even as doubts and obstacles rose in her mind, the firm pressure of his hand on hers flicked sparks of excitement through her body.

When she'd stalked out of the villa she'd been absolutely sure of what she was doing.

When he'd stumbled into the airport, she'd still been sure.

When he'd handed her that velvet box she'd thought, *Here we go again—he's going to try and buy his way out of trouble.*

And then he'd given her that old rusty key, splintering her jaded expectations and piquing her curiosity.

Material goods didn't interest her much, mostly because she knew they were easy to come by for him.

But this was something different. *He* was different.

And this new Cristiano was infinitely more dangerous than the old one because she had no idea how to handle him. When he was on the attack, she attacked right back. When he was arrogant and controlling, she wielded her own brand of power and took him on. But this Cristiano—this humble, penitent, remorseful Cristiano was a person she hadn't met before.

Confused, she looked away, thinking how unfair it was that the roughness of his jaw and his vaguely dishevelled appearance somehow made his dark Sicilian looks even more spectacular.

'Just because I'm sitting in this car, don't assume I've forgiven you.'

'I don't expect you to forgive me that easily.'

'Tell me what the key opens.'

A ghost of a smile touched that mouth. 'If I tell you that there is no reason for you to come with me. I'm relying on your inquisitive nature to provide the opportunity for me to show you how much I love you.'

He spoke the words easily. He always had, she remembered. For months, she'd struggled to get them past her lips whereas he'd experienced no such barriers to expressing himself.

But, in the end, that love hadn't revealed itself in his actions.

And now?

She stared down at the key in her lap. 'I promised myself that I wasn't going to do this. I promised myself that no matter what you said or did, I wasn't going to change my mind.'

All she'd cared about was protecting herself from more pain and yet somehow here she was, back in his car and in his life, cocooned by expensive leather and the smell of luxury with that dangerous, incendiary chemistry threatening everything she'd worked so hard to leave behind.

If he'd released her hand it might have helped, but he didn't. His fingers were wrapped hard around hers as he started the engine, and she knew he was fully aware of what his touch did to her and had no compunction in exploiting that advantage shamelessly.

Despairing of herself, Laurel leaned her head back against the seat. 'Give me one reason why I should do this.'

'Because I deserve another chance.' The engine gave a deep, throaty growl. 'Because what we have is special enough to keep fighting for.'

Was it?

Finally he released her hand but only so that he could place his on the wheel and steer them out of the nightmare traffic that clogged the airport road.

Whether this was a good idea or not, it was too late to rethink it because he found a gap in the traffic, pressed his foot to the floor and sped out of the airport.

CHAPTER SEVEN

CRISTIANO drove fast, skilfully dodging the heavy morning traffic until the road cleared. He pressed his foot to the floor and the car shot forward like a racehorse towards the finishing line, lightning-fast. Laurel smiled slightly as she felt the burst of speed and power because she loved it as much as he did.

Or maybe it was just because the top of the car was down and the sun was shining down on them, making everything impossible seem possible.

It was all still there, of course—the doubts, the worry and that other nagging emotion that he knew nothing about. But right now, with the breeze lifting her hair and the sun warming her face, she could push it to the back of her mind.

She wouldn't have admitted it in a million years, but she loved to watch him drive. Loved the confidence with which he handled the car, the subtle movement of his fingers as he shifted gears, the flex of powerful thigh muscle as he urged the car forward. Cristiano made driving a car sexy. To her, everything he did was sexy and that incurable attraction had always been her downfall.

Dragging her eyes away from temptation, Laurel anchored her hair with her hand and glanced over her shoulder. 'No security?'

'I think I may have run them over when I left the villa. I was in a hurry.' His swift smile managed to be disarming and devastating at the same time. 'Don't worry. I'm capable of protecting you and anyway, there is security where we are going.'

'Oh.' Her hopes of staying somewhere discreet and private dashed by that revelation, Laurel tried not to feel disappointed that there would be other people around. 'Where *are* we going?'

'It's a surprise. But you can trust me to have your happiness at the forefront of my list of priorities.'

She could have pointed out that her happiness had been right at the bottom of his list of priorities in the past but she could see he was trying so she bit her tongue and said nothing.

'Have I been there before?'

'Not exactly.'

Resigned to the fact that he wasn't going to reveal anything before he was ready, she leaned her head back against the seat and just watched the countryside. 'We're driving towards Mount Etna. You're going to drop me into the crater of an active volcano and finish me off for good?'

'Tempting.' The corners of his mouth flickered. 'And yes, we're driving towards Mount Etna.'

Her eyes fastened on the peak in the distance. 'I've always loved this part of Sicily.'

'I know.' They were off the *autostrade* now and climbing upwards, the car waltzing round the bends under Cristiano's expert control.

'Taormina?' Her heart gave a little jump as she realised where they were going. 'You're taking me to Taormina?' It was the place they'd spent part of their honeymoon and she'd been dizzy with the romance of the place. Yes, it was a favourite tourist haunt but with good reason. It was stunning.

The medieval town that had inspired poets and authors for centuries perched on the cliff whilst beneath lay the sparkling perfection of the Mediterranean, its surface reflecting all the colours of a peacock's wing.

As the sea breeze lifted her hair and cooled her skin, Laurel's smile faltered. 'Are we going back to the same hotel?'

'No. I wish you'd trust me.'

'I'm trying.'

'Try harder.'

That was all he would say and she held her breath as he negotiated a narrow road, one side of which fell into an almost vertical drop down to the sea.

This was Sicily at its most spectacular, mountains and sea coming together in dramatic perfection and there, carved into the hillside, was the Teatro Greco, the ruins of the ancient Greek theatre that was one of the most famous archaeological sites in Sicily.

It was the most breathtakingly seductive place she'd ever visited.

Leaving Taormina behind them, he drove on and Laurel was just coping with the thud of disappointment that this wasn't their destination after all when he stopped the car by a pair of tall, imposing iron gates. All around them were dark cypresses, olive trees and pines. Orange and lemon trees filled the air with their unforgettable Mediterranean scent and for a moment she closed her eyes and breathed deeply.

Even without looking she would have known she was in Sicily.

'Do you have that key?'

Roused by his voice, Laurel opened her eyes and stared at the gates and then at the key on her lap. 'This key opens those gates?'

'Try it and see.'

She stepped out of the car, feeling the sun burning her head. The jeans she'd worn to travel back to foggy London were too hot for this climate and suddenly she couldn't wait to change into something cooler. Without the movement of the car to cool the air it was baking hot, the ground dry and parched from the lack of rain.

Despite the less than encouraging volume of rust

clinging to the handle, the key slid joyfully into the lock but before she could turn it the gates started to open.

The car inched forwards behind her. 'I admit that I added a few mod cons,' Cristiano confessed, his smile apologetic. 'The key is symbolic rather than essential. Get back in. It's too hot to walk.'

'Walk where?' But Laurel climbed back into the car, noticing for the first time the security cameras above the gates. And then they were driving down a dusty lane bordered by olive groves and almond trees that she suspected had been there for centuries.

Here the air was scented with mimosa and jasmine and the sun beamed down on them as if smiling on their choice of destination.

Intrigued, Laurel glanced at Cristiano but his eyes were on the lane as he carefully negotiated the uneven surface. 'As you can see, this is a work in progress.' Grimacing as he picked his route, skilfully protecting the undercarriage of the car, he finally pulled up in a shaded courtyard.

Laurel's jaw dropped as she saw the magnificent honey-hued building. 'It's a castle?'

'Welcome to Castello di Vicario. The east part was built as a monastery in the twelfth century but the monks were booted out by a Sicilian prince with big ambitions who expanded it to house all his mistresses.' Cristiano leaned back and stared at the building with satisfaction. A profusion of Mediterranean flowers snaked up the walls and cascaded down from balconies, tumbled in colourful bursts against the sun-baked stone. 'Because of the views and the seclusion, it was used by artists and writers from all over Europe.'

'But who owns it now?'

'We do.' With that simple response, Cristiano sprang from the car and greeted the two Dobermanns who bounded from nowhere.

Laurel gasped as she saw the dogs, suddenly understanding his remark about already having security. 'Oh.' She was out of the car in a flash and down on her knees in the dust, hugging the dogs, laughing and crying as they licked her and greeted her with the same dopey enthusiasm she showed towards them. Within seconds she was covered in dust and paw prints but she didn't care.

When they were first married she'd hated the level of security he'd insisted on but the one compromise she'd been prepared to make was the dogs. With his customary wry humour he'd called them Rambo and Terminator and she'd taken them everywhere with her whenever she left the security of his offices in the hotel. Losing the dogs had been another reason she'd been broken-hearted to leave the island.

Cristiano watched with amusement as the dogs kicked up dust. 'Why didn't you ask me about them?'

'I didn't dare. I missed them so much—' She hugged Rambo tightly, pressing her face into his smooth black coat as he whined his pleasure at seeing her again. 'I couldn't bear hearing that you'd sold them or something.'

'I would never have sold them.' There was an odd expression on his face as he watched her.

'No, I don't suppose you would.' She played the pouncing game with Terminator as he barked for attention. 'They're far too valuable.'

'That isn't why.' His gaze enigmatic, he gestured to the door. 'Are you interested in seeing your home?'

Home?

'This is where you live now?' She rose slowly to her feet, one hand still on Terminator's head. The significance of it wasn't lost on her. Taormina was their place. It was the place they'd shared their first kiss. The place where he'd first told her that he loved her.

All the best parts of their relationship had been played out in this exquisite corner of the island. They'd strolled hand in hand along flower-decked streets, they'd enjoyed leisurely meals in one of the many intimate piazzas, but nowhere they'd stayed had been as perfect as this. As private, as exclusive—*as romantic.* 'When did you buy it?'

'I bought it while we were married but it needed a lot of attention. It was supposed to be a surprise.'

The shock of it made her heart skip a beat. '*While we were married?*'

'It was my gift to you. From the moment I saw how much you loved the place I wanted to find somewhere. It took me eighteen months to persuade the owners to sell. Another six months to make the necessary alterations.' He breathed deeply. 'And then you left.' The raw emotion in his voice brought the lump back to her throat and her eyes met his.

When he held out his hand, she hesitated because voluntarily putting her hand into his felt like a big step and she wasn't sure she was ready to take it. She experienced a painful moment of indecision and then she slid her hand into his and heard him exhale slowly.

It was a huge leap of faith and he apparently understood that because his fingers closed tightly around hers as he led her round the side of the house to a terrace that overlooked the sea.

'So, what do you think? Does it meet with your approval?'

Laurel looked up at the *castello* and felt overawed by the beauty of it. His wealth had always been part of who he was, of course. It was impossible not to be aware of it, but it had never interested her particularly. She'd always thought there was nothing his wealth could buy that could move her.

Until now.

She turned her back and discovered that from the terrace she was looking at a one hundred and eighty degree view that took in the snow-covered peak of Mount Etna and the dazzling emerald sea of the bay of Naxos. And on the terrace itself, just metres from her feet, a series of infinity pools cut into the slope, each cascading into the one beneath, the insistent rush of water soothing in the humid heat of the day.

'I think you have delusions of grandeur,' she croaked and he laughed and pulled her into his arms in a possessive gesture, not giving her the chance to reject that spontaneous intimacy.

'The pools are inspired, don't you think? You always loved to swim so I told our architect to make use of the gradient to create something special. I always thought it was a good idea but I must admit it surpassed my vision.'

'You saw us living here?'

'Yes, for some of the time, at least. It was good enough for DH Lawrence and Truman Capote so it must have something special.'

Yes, it was special. Special in every way. But the most special thing about it was that he'd done this for her.

He'd done this for her while she'd been working the same punishing hours that he'd been working. She'd accused him of being a workaholic and now she was discovering that at least part of his working day had been devoted to building somewhere that she was going to love. Not somewhere he'd lived as a rich single guy but somewhere he'd chosen with her in mind.

Somewhere that was their own.

Her impression of him shifted into a different shape. Thoroughly confused and hating that feeling, she pulled away from him and he sighed.

'*Now* what's going through that head of yours? Tell me what you're thinking.'

She was thinking that this house, the fact he'd built it in the place she loved most on earth, was an enormous gesture. But it was a gesture with meaning. He'd built it for their future. For the family he'd imagined having. It was all part of his master plan. Looking at the olive groves, she imagined two small versions of Cristiano playing in the shade and then splashing in one of the beautiful turquoise pools.

Maybe he *had* loved her in his own way. Looking at what he'd created here, she was almost ready to believe that.

Which made the sense of loss even more painfully acute.

They ate lunch on a shaded part of the terrace, surrounded by the lavish gardens and fragrant citrus groves.

Laurel ate fish with lemon and herbs picked from the garden, her cheeks pale and her eyes tired as she pecked at her food. The dogs lay by her feet in a state of dopey adoration, refusing to leave her side as they panted in the heat.

And he was as bad as the dogs, Cristiano thought wryly as he waited for her to confide in him. He knew exactly what was on her mind. It didn't take a genius to guess and he could have raised it but he wanted to see if she would do it without his prompting.

Aware that confidences were hardly likely to be forthcoming when things were so tense between them, he chose to steer the conversation onto neutral territory. 'Where have you lived for the past two years?' He watched, hiding his concern as she toyed with the fish on her plate, her usually healthy appetite clearly challenged by their problems.

Would she tell him what was worrying her?

'I based myself in London.'

'You didn't touch a penny of your allowance in all the time we were apart.'

'I wasn't with you for the money, Cristiano.'

'I would have supported you financially. I made that commitment when we married.'

He waited for her to make a pointed remark about the commitments he hadn't made but she didn't.

'You're surrounded by people who are only interested in you for what you can give them and you're complaining because I didn't want that?'

'I wanted to provide for you.' And the strength

of that need shocked him because he'd always considered himself progressive for a Sicilian male.

'Ah.' Her eyes lifted to his. 'The Provider.'

The past hung between them and he was acutely aware that although he'd provided for her materially he'd neglected her shamefully on the one occasion she'd reached out to him.

And suddenly he knew with absolute certainty that there was a reason why this was such a hot button for her. It wasn't just that he, with his horrendously busy schedule and careless attitude had let her down shamefully, it was that he'd ripped open a wound that hadn't completely healed.

He knew that her childhood had been difficult, but she'd given him few details and he hadn't pressed. But suddenly he wanted to know who, or what, had caused the original wound.

The shrill tone of his phone disturbed the silence and Cristiano, pre-programmed to answer it promptly, automatically reached for it and then remembered his promise about priorities.

His hand froze in mid-air.

Swiftly recovering, hoping desperately that she hadn't noticed the detour his hand had taken from the glass in front of him to his pocket, he returned his attention to the woman seated opposite him. The phone continued to ring and Laurel raised an eyebrow.

'Are you going to answer that?'

'No.' It took a painful degree of willpower but somehow he managed not to reach into his pocket although his palms were sweating and his fingers were aching to just answer the damn thing.

It was a relief when it stopped ringing.

Observing his struggle, she put her fork down. 'Next time just answer it. You know you want to.'

Part of him *did* want to, but he recognised that as a habitual response derived from years of putting work first.

She'd called him 'the Provider' and Cristiano acknowledged the accuracy of that description. He'd slipped into that role from the moment he'd taken the distressed call from his mother on the day his father had died suddenly.

He'd left the US immediately, flown home and taken charge. And he'd been in that role ever since, even though his younger brother had long since proved himself capable of playing his part.

What had started as necessity had become a way of life and he'd never even questioned it.

Until now.

Now, the opportunity to close another deal, to expand the business, to make more profit were all subordinate to his need to make his marriage work. For possibly the first time in his life, he didn't care what the person on the phone wanted. He had no urge to check his voicemail. He didn't care if his business was collapsing.

The phone started ringing again, the shrill insistent tone disturbing the tranquillity of the terrace and sending the tiny sparrows swooping for cover. And all the time Laurel was watching him, those beautiful green eyes guarded.

'Answer it. Then you'll be able to stop wondering who it was and how much money you just lost by not taking the call.'

'That isn't what I'm wondering.' He was wondering how on earth he was going to compensate for what he'd done to her. How he was going to prove to her that he loved her.

What sort of provider had he been to Laurel? Financially, yes, he'd provided for her, but emotionally he'd left her to fend for herself and that knowledge scraped uncomfortably over his conscience.

'Did you even tell anyone where you were going?' She sounded exasperated. 'They're probably sending out a search party as we speak.'

'It's true that I haven't told anyone.'

'You've probably triggered a security alert.'

'Very possibly.' Remembering the startled faces of his security team, he breathed deeply, frustrated by the realities of his life. 'Perhaps I ought to just—'

'Yes. Do it!' She reached for her glass. 'I don't expect you not to work, Cristiano. You're missing the point. I have every intention of going through my own emails later. I respect your drive and ambition. I have plenty of it myself. That isn't a problem. That *wasn't* the problem.' Her change of tense took them swiftly to the heart of the real problem and it wasn't his phone, which had once again stopped ringing.

She sipped her water.

Sweat broke out on the back of his neck.

He was thinking, as she was, that he'd let her down when she'd needed him most. Images of her alone in that hospital bed kept flying into his head. 'If it is any consolation, I feel like an utter bastard for what I did to you.'

'You mean for what you *didn't* do.'

'That too.'

'Good. You should feel bad.' Slowly, she put her glass down on the table. 'You were thoughtless and insensitive.'

He winced as he recognised himself in that description. 'So you're not going to say, *Don't worry about it*?'

'No. You *should* worry about it. It was shocking behaviour. If you weren't worried I wouldn't be sitting here now.'

Cristiano wondered whether it was him or whether Sicily was in the grip of a searing heatwave. His palms were sweating—even his brain felt hot. When his phone rang for a third time he hauled it out of his pocket deciding that one conversation now would save a myriad of interruptions for the next few weeks.

'Five minutes,' he vowed as he scanned the number. 'It's Santo. I'll tell him he's in charge. Then I'm switching it off.'

Laurel was staring in astonishment. '*What* happened to your phone?'

'I had a slight accident. It fell out of my pocket when I was grabbing my clothes in a hurry to try and catch you at the airport.'

'Oh, dear.' Her eyes lifted to his. 'You *did* have a stressful morning.'

It had to be the understatement of the century. 'I've certainly had better.' The irony in his tone drew a hesitant smile from her.

'What would have happened if my flight had already taken off?'

Having contemplated that possibility for the whole of his crazy drive through Palermo, Cristiano had no wish to revisit those emotions. 'I would have had to make an impromptu visit to London, which would have been a shame,' he murmured, 'because I hear that you are having a particularly wet English summer. Fortunately, both of us have been spared that.'

'This is just temporary, Cristiano. I haven't agreed to anything.' Having delivered that less than encouraging reminder that the future of their relationship was still undecided, she glanced at the phone vibrating in his hand. 'You need a new one.'

'The state of my phone is the least of my worries right now.' It was the state of his marriage that troubled him. His challenge now was to work out how to gain her trust again. He understood that for Laurel, trust was everything.

'Answer it, before Santo decides that I've killed you and buried the body.'

Cristiano rose to his feet. 'This will be quick—' Without once taking his eyes off Laurel, he switched to Italian, giving his brother an edited version of the past few hours. When he hung up Laurel's gaze was steady.

'I expect he wanted to know whether you'd thrown me out yet.'

'He knows I'm still in love with you.' That declaration sent the tension rippling between them.

'I can't imagine that went down well.'

'I don't need my brother's permission for the way I feel.'

'He hates me, Cristiano. I saw his face yesterday. And your mother gave me a long reproachful look. I'm the evil daughter-in-law.' Her eyes tired, she pushed her chair back from the table and stood up. 'You can't pretend it doesn't matter. Nor can you punch everyone who says bad things about me. This place is beautiful, but it doesn't change the fact that we're a mess. Nothing can change that.' She turned abruptly and walked to the edge of the pool.

Knowing that there was more that she wasn't telling him, Cristiano strode after her and closed his hands over her shoulders.

Her arms were lean and strong but he could tell that she'd lost weight in the time they'd been apart and that knowledge was one more blow to his conscience.

'A mess can always be cleaned up and this isn't about anyone else. It's about us. I want you to relax. The last few days have been horrendous for you.' He thought of how she'd looked as she'd stepped off that plane, so brave and gutsy as she'd walked into hell so that she could be by the side of her best friend.

And he, instead of admiring her courage, had questioned her loyalty.

'Stop thinking and worrying and sending black looks in my direction and just enjoy your favourite place on earth. This evening I'm taking you down to a restaurant I've discovered on the beach. Just locals, so far undiscovered by tourists.' They were going to spend time together, he vowed. Time they hadn't spent together after they were married.

There was a moment when neither of them spoke and then she drew in a little breath.

'I don't have anything to wear.'

That quintessentially female response loosened the tension in his muscles. If her biggest worry was what she was going to wear then they were making progress. 'That is easily fixed. There are clothes in the dressing room.'

Her head turned. Those beautiful eyes cooled and

narrowed. 'Your bedroom is stocked with women's clothes?'

'*Our* bedroom.' He found that uncensored display of female jealousy oddly reassuring. At least she cared who he'd been clothing in her absence. 'I bought them for you. It was part of the surprise. The day after we discovered you were pregnant you went to London on business and I made all the final arrangements. When you landed in Sicily I was going to bring you here.'

'Instead of which you flew off to the Caribbean and we didn't even see each other.'

Another regret to add to the pile already littering his mind. 'Yes.'

'I only saw you once more after that, when I was packing to leave Sicily.' She paused. 'I expected you to come after me. Not that I wanted you to, but I expected it. Why didn't you?'

It was a question he'd asked himself a million times. 'I was blinded by my own sense of righteous injustice that you'd walked out on our marriage. I made many mistakes. Give me the chance to make it up to you.'

There was a long silence. 'Can we go for a walk through the town? I always loved the little antique shops and the buzz.'

At that moment he realised just how afraid he'd been that she'd demand to be taken back to the airport. That she wouldn't give him another chance.

'It's the middle of the day, *tesoro*. You will be sautéed in the heat and squashed by tourists.'

'I'm sure you have a hat in the wardrobe you bought me and the two of us can elbow our way through tourists. Please? I really want to do something normal.'

Normal?

'There's nothing normal about choosing to walk along the Corso Umberto in the heat of the sun.' *Especially when I want to take you to bed, undress you and explore every inch of you.*

But that part of their relationship had always been easy.

It was the rest of it that had proved challenging.

And it was the rest of it he was determined to fix.

They strolled through the old medieval town, exploring the network of narrow streets and alleyways. To the casual observer they probably looked like lovers enjoying a holiday but Laurel was aware that his attentiveness sprang not from the romance of their surroundings but from a genuine desire to heal the deep rift between them.

Whether or not it could be healed, she didn't know.

Putting her trust in someone had taken a huge leap of faith on her part. And he'd let her fall. She wasn't sure she was ready to risk doing it again.

A pretty bikini caught her eye in the window of

an exclusive boutique and she went to try it on, eager for distraction from her own thoughts.

She hadn't had a proper holiday for years, she realised as she looked at her reflection in the mirror. Not since their honeymoon. After that they'd both been sucked into the volume of work that demanded their attention. It would be bliss to just spend some time lying by that beautiful pool with a book. If she could relax for long enough.

This wasn't a holiday, was it?

It was—

She frowned as she realised she didn't really know what it was. A reconciliation? A trial of togetherness? Was it possible to fix what had gone wrong between them? She didn't know. What she *did* know was that she wasn't the same girl he'd married.

Wondering whether he'd still be interested in the person she was now, she handed the bikini to the girl behind the desk. Cristiano insisted on paying and she let him because she knew it would please him to spoil her and it seemed petty to argue over something so small.

As he handed over his credit card Laurel saw the girl send him furtive glances and turn a pretty shade of pink.

Even dressed casually, he had that effect on women, she thought. And most of the time he wasn't even aware of it. Or maybe it just happened so frequently he no longer noticed.

As they left the shop, Laurel glanced over her shoulder and sighed when she caught the girl staring enviously after her. 'That girl was ready to marry you and have your babies.' She spoke without thinking and Cristiano frowned.

'What girl?'

'The one in the shop.'

'I'm already married. And I'm staying that way.'

He didn't tackle the other part of her sentence and Laurel wondered what on earth had possessed her to make a remark like that. What had she been thinking? And what was the point of this attempt at reconciliation, because even if they managed to fix one part of this mess, there was another part that couldn't be changed.

With one glance at her stricken face, Cristiano took charge. He tightened his grip on her hand and led her purposefully down a narrow side street that was shady and relatively free of people.

'All right, enough,' he breathed, backing her against the stone wall of an ancient church and trapping her with his arms. 'Right from the moment you told me what happened I have been waiting for you to raise the issue that is worrying you, but as usual you've kept it to yourself. I have to sit there watching while you pick at your lunch, growing paler and paler while your mind spins reasons for us not to be together.'

'I don't know what you're talking about.'

'Babies. You are thinking, *There is no point in fixing this because I can't have children and he won't want me if I can't have children.*'

It was a part truth and Laurel felt the sharp sting of tears behind her eyes because the whole truth was so much more complicated than that.

He had no idea.

Alarmed by her own emotional reaction, she blinked rapidly. She was just tired. Really tired.

'So you're a mind-reader now?'

'Are you telling me I'm wrong?'

'No.' But it wasn't all of it. Despite the searing heat, a chill washed over her. 'It's one more barrier between us, that's for sure.'

'*Not* to me.' His accent was suddenly more pronounced than usual, his eyes a deep, intense shade of black as he looked at her with fierce intensity. 'I love you. I have some work to do to prove it to you, but I *do* love you. And I am sorry that I wasn't with you when you received that news. I can't even imagine how you must have felt.'

Laurel didn't enlighten him.

It was too soon for a conversation of that depth, particularly when she knew that her feelings on that subject would probably shock him.

'I should have been there to support you,' he said quietly. 'I'm not surprised you walked out on me.'

It was the first time he'd admitted that her response might have been justified.

'I didn't do it to punish you. I did it because I decided I was better on my own. Safer.'

His hands lifted to her shoulders and she felt the strength in them as they tightened. 'Safer?'

'I was protecting myself.'

That admission drew a frown from him. 'From me?'

'From hurt. It's instinctive.'

'I know. I've learned that about you. But I wish you'd just shouted at me instead of walking out. I wish you'd lost your temper and told me how you felt.'

'Telling you wouldn't have changed anything. I didn't leave because I was angry with you. I left because I knew I couldn't trust you again. I didn't dare.' She felt the tension ripple through his hard frame and he pulled her closer, the contact sending a spasm of awareness through her body. The physical side of their relationship had clouded everything else and it was having that same effect now. And she knew he was feeling it too because when he spoke his voice was raw and rough.

'And now? Are you willing to take that chance?'

'I don't know.'

'Because you don't trust me not to let you down again or because of the children thing?'

'Both. You want children. That's a fact. We talked about it often and your mother asked me on a daily basis when I was going to give you babies.' Laurel tried to pull away from him but he gave a rough curse and pulled her back into the curve of his arms, resting his chin on her head.

'*Mi dispiace*, I'm sorry. That was insensitive of her and I had no idea. I will speak to her.'

'It's what she wants for you.' Her voice was muffled against his chest and he held her, oblivious to the tourists strolling past them. They watched with idle curiosity, no doubt wondering what the spectacularly handsome Sicilian man was saying to the dark haired girl in his arms.

'Let's just deal with the whole children thing right now because it is clouding the real issue here. Answer me something honestly—' Gently, he stroked her hair away from her face. 'If it had been me who couldn't have children would you have left me?'

'Of course not!' It was a reasonable question but she knew it wasn't the relevant one. 'It isn't the same.'

'It's *exactly* the same.'

'No. It's more complicated than that.' Although she could have stayed like that for ever, she eased away because this was a conversation that needed to be completed. 'Perhaps it's easier for me because

I didn't grow up dreaming of families and children. I didn't have those ambitions. I suppose I just didn't believe in happy endings. But you did.'

'I wouldn't describe it as an ambition. More of an assumption. And if you think that what you just told me would change the way I feel about you then you truly have no idea how much I love you.' His voice was decidedly unsteady. 'Which means I still have a great deal to prove.'

'I don't want you to jump through hoops, Cristiano—' This time she did pull away from him. 'I don't even know if we have a future together. You're asking me to take a leap of faith and I'm not sure I can do that, especially after what I've just told you. It's huge.'

'Compared to losing you, it's minuscule.'

She didn't know whether it was his husky voice or the look in his eyes, but the tense little knot inside her unravelled and she realised that no matter what she said or did she would always love this man and the depth of that love would always make her vulnerable.

'It's not just you.' Admitting it was hard. 'It's me. I'm just not good at relationships. I'm not sure if I can give you what you want from me.'

'Because of what I did to you two years ago? Or because of what someone else did to you years before that?' His gentle tone smoothed the edges of the blunt words, his gaze fixed on hers as he broached a subject she'd carefully dodged for the whole time they'd been together. 'Yes, I behaved badly and you have every right to be angry with me but your trust issues didn't begin with me.'

And he was right, of course. Her trust issues, her refusal to depend on others, had begun years before she'd met him. They were fossilised into the foundations of who she was.

When she didn't answer, he sighed. 'I know your life was hell as a child and that you learned never to trust anyone, but I'm telling you that you *can* trust me. I messed up, but that wasn't because I didn't love you. I was crazy about you. I adored every independent inch of you. Yes, I made a bad judgement but even that wasn't quite as straightforward as it seemed because the situation was complicated. Now *stop* thinking and worrying and let's just go home and spend some time together.' Lacing his fingers into hers, he led her back onto the main street that led towards Piazza Sant'Antonio.

'By "spend some time together" I assume you mean have sex.'

'That wasn't what I meant. That's the one area of our relationship that has never needed any attention.' He paused to kiss her, indifferent to whoever might have been watching, the touch of his mouth a sensual reminder of what they'd shared the night before.

Her head spun and she wondered dimly whether

this whole thing would have been easier if the sexual attraction between them hadn't been so extraordinarily powerful.

'I can't think when you do that.'

'Good.' His slumberous gaze moved to her mouth. 'You think far too much.'

Right now all she could think about was sex. And she could tell by the way those heavy-lidded eyes darkened that he was thinking the same thing. In fact she knew he was because when she started to move he caught her hips and pulled a face.

'*Don't* move for a minute.'

Because he was usually the one with all the control, it was fun to tease him. 'What happens if I move?'

His teeth were gritted. 'I'll probably be arrested for indecency. Stand still. And stop looking at me like that.'

She licked her bottom lip slowly and heard him mutter something in Italian. 'I didn't understand that.'

'Probably just as well.' He exhaled slowly and stepped away from her. 'Let's get back home quickly. Move.'

CHAPTER EIGHT

LAUREL lay naked in a warm after-sex glow, her limbs tangled with Cristiano's as they watched the sun set over Mount Etna, turning the sky a deep rosy gold.

'It's as if the island's on fire.' *Like their relationship*, she thought. If their love were a colour, it would have been red. Red for hot. Red for passion.

He rolled her onto her back. 'Not just the island.' He lowered his head and immediately she was consumed by the hungry demands of his kiss.

Red for desire.

She felt her own heart pounding and the thrill of excitement mount as his hand stroked down over her thigh in a smooth, possessive movement.

Being with Cristiano was the ultimate adrenalin rush, an experience of such erotic intensity that her senses were constantly humming.

'Did you really not have an affair?' She hated herself for asking, for sounding like someone needy and insecure when she'd always prided herself on her independence but part of her—*the part she wished she could dig out and throw away*—couldn't stop torturing herself with that scenario.

He went utterly still. 'Do you have any idea what my life was like after you left?'

'Awkward. I expect a lot of people told you I was a heartless woman and you were well shot of me.'

The flash in his eyes told her how close to the mark she was with that comment and it hurt. He saw the hurt because he was looking for it. 'I've never been interested in other people's opinions.'

'I imagined you slowly working your way through layers deep of admirers.'

'You imagined?' His hand slid into her hair, his jaw tight as he scanned her tense features. 'That imagination of yours needs retraining. After you left, the only relationship I had was with the business, apart from the occasional flirtation with the whisky bottle. Reality was me working an eighteen-hour day in the hope that when I eventually fell into bed I'd be too tired to think about you.' That frank admission made her heart lift.

He'd missed her.

'Did it work?'

'No. But we had two record years.' His eyes gleamed dark with self-mockery. 'Company profits have trebled.'

'So—'

'No, I didn't.' His voice harsh, he slid his hand under her bottom. 'Did you?'

'No.'

'Even anger and pain doesn't kill love, apparently. I was so angry that you'd walked out on our marriage I didn't go any deeper than that. If I had, we might have reached this point sooner.' This point was his hands and mouth claiming her, driving her wild until she forgot everything except the magic they created together.

In the aftermath of another sexual explosion, she lay still, her cheek against his chest, her hair spread over the pillow.

This, she thought, *was the part they'd been good at.*

The part they hadn't been so good at was the rest of it. And the responsibility for that didn't all rest with him, she acknowledged. She'd been at fault too. She'd guarded herself. She'd been afraid to let him in. She hadn't even considered such a thing as second chances.

Had she been unfair?

And what about now?

She knew that he was waiting for her to say, *I love you.* And she couldn't. She just wasn't ready.

The past hung between them, an obstacle to everything, including her ability to confide and his ability to understand her.

'It wasn't all your fault.' Her cheek was against

his shoulder, her hand resting low on his stomach. 'I expect people to let me down so it's better not to trust them in the first place.'

'I *did* let you down.'

'But I gave you one chance.' The thought that she'd been too harsh knocked the breath from her lungs but his arms tightened as if he sensed her confusion.

'You were protecting yourself. I understand that. You've been let down so badly in the past and I let you down again.'

The sting of guilt about her own part in their break up made her speak. 'I've been there before. I've felt the excitement, the hope—that warm feeling of belonging that comes when you think someone wants you to be with them. And when that went wrong, when I wasn't what they wanted me to be, I hurt so badly I promised myself that I wasn't going to let it happen again.'

His hand stilled. 'Are we talking about a man?'

Knowing how possessive he was, it was to his credit that his grip on her didn't slacken.

'You were the first man I'd slept with. You know that.'

'Then who? Who hurt you?' His voice was rough. 'Talk to me.'

It was obvious that he wanted answers. And he deserved that much, didn't he? 'When I was little I was almost adopted.'

'Almost?' He was puzzled and of course he would be because someone like him would have no reason to know that it was even possible to be 'almost' adopted.

'When I was in care a couple visited me several times. They thought I might be "the one". They'd wanted a baby, but there was no baby and at least I was a girl. They really wanted a girl. For ten years they'd been trying to have their own. Spent a fortune on IVF and then turned to adoption and found that too many years had passed and now they were too old to be given a baby. They'd even prepared the house—done up a room especially. Painted it all in pink with tiny fairy lights. They needed a child to match the room and their dreams. They thought I was that child. I wasn't blonde and blue-eyed, but I got to spend a weekend with them. They took me home.' Remembering was hard, even after so many years. She remembered the perfume the woman had worn and her perfect clothes. Two cars in the driveway and space, so much space. 'I didn't care about all the pink, but I cared about the books. You should have seen the books.' She could still picture them clearly in her head, rows of books, colourful spines facing outwards, as attractive as jars of sweets in a sweet shop. 'Children's books, fairy stories—everything. I'd never had a book of my own when I was young. Never read a fairy story in my life. And this couple loved books. He was an English teacher and she worked in a florists. There were books and flowers everywhere. And they picked me. They wanted me. I was so excited.'

'You went to live with them?'

Pulling away from him, she rolled onto her back. 'No. That first night staying with them I was so stressed at being in a strange place with strange people I really couldn't breathe. I had an asthma attack. We spent the whole time in the emergency department, and after that—' she paused, surprised that memories so old could still feel so new '—after that they decided that it was better to be childless than have me. They didn't sign up for a sick child, midnight dashes to the emergency department, worry and anxiety. They wanted a child who was going to fit into that room, all golden curls, pink dresses and everything perfect. I wasn't that person—which was a shame because I'd fallen in love with the room. Not the pink, but the books. I loved the idea of having a door I could shut with all the books on the inside. I was going to pretend it was a library. I was going to read every single one and it was going to be an adventure.' Conscious that she'd revealed more than she'd intended, she lightened the tone as she turned her head to look at him. 'So now you know why I'm such a mess. No books.' And no family, but she didn't mention that part. Didn't mention the devastation and sense of rejection that had followed that traumatic experience. 'Maybe if I'd read a few fairy tales I wouldn't be such a disaster. The trouble is, I wouldn't know a happy ending if I fell over it.'

The silence stretched between them and Cristiano raised himself on his elbow so that he could look at her. His eyes were dark pools of appalled disbelief. 'You're saying they changed their minds?'

'It happens. That's why they did a trial. It's important that the adoption process is right for everyone. I wasn't right for them.' And that shouldn't still hurt, should it? 'It was hard for me because I was very young and I let myself trust them. When they said I was going to be their little girl, I believed them, which was stupid really because I already knew that adults usually didn't mean what they said.'

His face was paler than usual. 'And after that?'

'After that I pretty much made myself unadoptable. It was better for everyone that way.'

'Because you didn't want to risk it happening again.' His voice husky, he reached out and stroked her hair away from her face. 'How old were you?'

'Eight.' She saw his expression change. 'I was eight years old. But I'd spent all of those eight years between foster homes and care homes so I wasn't your average eight-year-old.' She felt his arms wrap around her and then he was pulling her against him again, and this time his grip was that much tighter.

'Why didn't you tell me this before?'

'I try not to think about it. It's in the past. It isn't

relevant.' Even as she said the words she knew they weren't true. And so did he.

'We both know it's relevant. It's the reason you protect yourself so fiercely. It explains a lot.' His arms tightened possessively as if he wanted to make up for all those years of isolation and loneliness.

'You're right. It does still affect me in that it has influenced who I am. Because of that I made up my mind that the only person I was going to depend on was myself. I didn't really have close friends because I didn't trust anyone enough to form a bond.'

'You made friends with Dani.'

'Technically, she made friends with me. We were in the same accommodation at college and she's like you—she's so emotionally open, she won't take no for an answer. Every time I closed the door to my room, she opened it. She was always dragging me out to various events. She wouldn't let me hide and truthfully I loved her company. She was the first real friend I'd had. And she never let me down.' Laurel's eyes filled. 'When I left you she should have ended our friendship, but she didn't. She wouldn't.'

'My sister is fantastic, but don't tell her I said that.' Humour lightened the roughness of his voice and the hand that stroked her hair was gentle. 'It's no wonder that you left after what I did. And I know that this is a mess but we can fix it. We *will* fix it. I won't accept a different option.'

'What if we can't? I'm so afraid of being let down

it colours everything I do.' It felt so good to be this close to him again that she couldn't concentrate on anything else. It would have been frighteningly easy to just close her eyes and let him decide for both of them. 'Once you trust someone they hold the power to hurt you.'

Strong hands flipped her on her back and he covered her with the lean, muscular length of his body. 'I love you. I messed up badly but you're going to forgive me because you love me too. And it isn't because you don't love me that you're hesitating, it's because you're afraid.'

'I know.'

'And you can get over that. You're the toughest, strongest woman I know. I can't believe how you've coped with so much on your own. That awful day two years ago—I wasn't listening to you properly,' he confessed in a raw tone. 'You rang me and you told me you were worried but the doctor had already told me he thought you'd be fine so half my mind—more than half my mind if I'm honest—was on the business deal I was trying to close. It is no defence, but it was something I'd been working on for five years. Had I known how frightened you were, I would have dropped everything and come.'

'I was terrified.'

He gave a groan of remorse and rolled onto his back, taking her with him. His hand was in her hair, his eyes holding hers. 'I wish I could rewind the clock and do things differently. You have no idea how much I wish that.'

'It wouldn't change anything. You wouldn't have jeopardised a deal for me, Cristiano.'

'My marriage was more important than any deal but at the time I didn't realise it was a choice. I didn't realise just how important it was to you that I be there. It's no excuse but the doctor *did* assure me that you would be fine.'

His eyes were beautiful, she thought. Or perhaps it was his eyelashes that were beautiful. Dense and inky-black, they framed a gaze that read her all too easily. Most men were emotionally inarticulate but Cristiano was the exception. He had no trouble expressing his feelings and no problem interpreting hers. His emotional sophistication far exceeded hers. Which made his response to her desperate plea for him to be there all the more out of character.

If he'd been distracted then it must have been a major distraction. 'Why was that deal so important to you?'

'It doesn't matter now. There are no excuses for the way I behaved.'

'Tell me about the deal, Cristiano.'

He lay still, and then he sighed and sat up, raking one hand through his hair. 'It goes without saying that it came at the worst time. Five years of work that came to a head the day before you flew back from London. I'd planned for us both to have dinner. Instead you were flying in and I was flying out.'

Too late she remembered that he'd been preoccupied on the phone—that he'd barely responded the first time she'd tentatively mentioned that she thought something might be wrong.

'What was so important about that particular deal?'

He stared down at his hands and gave a bitter laugh. 'You ask me that now and I can't even remember. It was another prime piece of land that would have been perfect for an exclusive resort hotel. More of what I already do. Except that this was bigger than anything we'd dealt with and I wanted it badly. I knew that owning that island would secure the future of the company and our reputation at the top end of the business.'

'Was the company in trouble?'

'No, but no business that majors in tourism can afford to be complacent. The whole market is volatile. That's another reason we operate at the expensive end.' His bronzed back was sleek and smooth, the muscles in those shoulders a blatant declaration of his physical power. 'You accused me of being a workaholic and you're right. That is what I am.'

Laurel remembered what Dani had said about him having held everything together after their father had died. 'I suppose you had to be. You found yourself in control of everything at a young age.'

'Everything?' His laughter lacked humour. 'If we're talking about the business then "everything" amounted to two small hotels which barely scraped a profit.'

'I thought it was your father's business?'

'What I have now grew out of my father's business.' He stared through the open doors to the prettily lit terrace and the turquoise-blue shimmer of the infinity pool. 'I was at college when my father died and suddenly I was in charge, thrown into the middle of something I knew nothing about. My mother was devastated, my brother and sister were still at school. My father owned two hotels on the island, neither of them doing that well. I was the oldest son. I was studying structural engineering, but that was irrelevant. Everyone was depending on me.'

And he'd only been in his very early twenties, she calculated. Studying in the US on the brink of his own adventure.

How much had it taken to give all that up and return home to continue his father's dreams instead of pursuing his own?

'What started as necessity became a habit. After a while I didn't even question why I was working so hard. It was just the way I lived my life. It didn't matter how much money I made or how successful the business became, I couldn't forget that everyone was depending on me. On my ability to expand and grow the company.'

And he hadn't just been supporting his mother and siblings, Laurel realised, but employing huge numbers of his family. Not just his brother and sister but several cousins and two uncles.

They'd made him the Provider.

They'd leaned on him, and he'd braced his powerful shoulders and taken on that role.

'Carlo advised me to walk away from the Caribbean deal because the price they were demanding just didn't make it a viable proposition. We were about to give up when they came back with a counter-offer. We had twenty-four hours to make a decision on whether to go ahead or not. I thought that deal would secure the future of the company. It was a recession-proof investment.'

'So you went ahead?' She hadn't questioned what had happened to the business after she'd walked out.

'Yes. And it's doing well. Better than even I predicted.' He turned his head to look at her. 'But Carlo was right about one thing. The price *was* too high.'

She knew he wasn't talking about the financial implications. 'I was selfish,' she muttered. 'I didn't think about your responsibility to everyone else. I only thought about my needs.'

'With reason.'

'I thought, *It's just another business deal*. I never thought about the pressure on you. I never once thought about all the people depending on you for employment. You never talked to me about it.'

'I didn't want to talk about work when I was with you. I was crazy about you. I'm still crazy about you.' His tone was rough and decidedly unsteady. 'I've been crazy about you since the first day I saw you in your running shorts, shouting at Santo for slacking.'

There was no mistaking his sincerity and her heart stopped because she realised how badly she'd misunderstood the situation. 'On our wedding day, I believed that you loved me. Whenever I was with you, I believed you. But we were together less and less. By the time I discovered that I was pregnant, we were spending virtually no time together. The fact that you didn't come when I asked you to was the final straw. I saw it as evidence that you didn't love me.'

'I thought marrying you proved how much I loved you. I committed that cardinal male sin of taking too much for granted.' He leaned forward and kissed her mouth gently. 'It's possible that I was a touch arrogant.'

'Possible?' She smiled against his lips because that statement said everything about his own healthy sense of self-worth. 'And that single gesture—marrying me—was supposed to last me a lifetime?'

He eased back from her. 'I wasn't as bad as that. I gave you daily proof of my love for you. I sent you endless gifts.'

'Actually, your PA sent me endless gifts,' Laurel

murmured. 'Do you think I didn't know that you said, "Send my wife flowers", and she arranged it?'

'I *chose* you jewellery.'

'From a selection sent to your office to minimise the inconvenience and generally reduce the impact on your working day. I'm not saying you weren't generous,' she said hastily. 'I'm just saying that none of those things made me feel secure.'

'They should have done. They were supposed to.'

'Why? They weren't personal. They were generic gifts. Gifts that had probably earned you undying gratitude in the past but to me they had no meaning except to remind me that you're a very wealthy man. And that there is a whole harem of women out there just waiting to exploit the first crack in our marriage. Are you seriously telling me that I was the first woman you have ever given jewellery to?'

He cast her an incredulous glance because this was a topic they'd never really touched on and he clearly didn't think they should be touching on it now. 'No, I'm not telling you that. But you were the first and only woman I have ever loved.'

'And I was supposed to just know that.'

'Yes, but I didn't know how badly you'd been let down. Had you told me—'

'I would have made myself even more emotionally vulnerable.'

'A little more insight into the workings of your mind might have prevented me from getting things so badly wrong. *Not* that I'm blaming you for my failings.'

'I admit that my past experience has made me cautious and I can't do anything about that but I didn't see anything when we were together to make me think that I was that important to you. Gradually you spent more and more time at work.' She curled her legs up, feeling vulnerable just talking about it. 'And then I reached out to you. And you didn't have time for me. I wasn't a priority and that convinced me you didn't love me. And that is why I left, Cristiano. That is why I never had the confidence that our relationship could survive. You never gave me any indication that it could.'

And part of her—that horrid part of her that she hated so much—still wouldn't let her just take his declaration of love and believe in it without question. She wished it could have been that easy and for a million other women it probably would have been. To hear Cristiano Ferrara say 'I love you' had been the pinnacle of ambition for many women.

For her, they were just words.

Frustrated with herself, Laurel slid off the bed, wrapped herself in a robe and walked onto the terrace. The fact that he let her go so easily told her a great deal about the way he was feeling now that the depth of her insecurities had been exposed.

Fear was a cold, creeping sensation over her heated skin because she understood finally that the future of their marriage relied not on her ability to bear children, but her ability to trust him not to hurt her.

What did she mean, he'd never given her any indication?

Cristiano lay back on the bed, hands hooked behind his head, thinking back over the two years of their marriage and forcing himself to confront some uncomfortable facts.

He'd bought her jewellery. Flowers. Extravagant gifts that he'd believed had demonstrated the depth of his feelings. All arranged via the efficient channels that she'd so astutely identified.

The thought made him squirm.

She'd always thanked him, but what time and effort had he put into those gifts? He'd given her what he thought she wanted instead of what she really wanted and the harsh truth of that shamed him.

Guilt, an almost familiar companion since she'd arrived back in Sicily, was sharp and painful.

What thought had he given to any of it? He'd treated her the way he'd treated previous women in his life who had measured every gift by its monetary value. But expensive gifts from a wealthy man meant nothing to a woman like Laurel, who had been building her own business and was justifiably proud of her success. She hadn't wanted financial security. She'd never been interested in him for his money. What she'd needed was emotional security and he, in all his arrogance, had never given her that. She'd thirsted for some demonstration of his love and he, with the same arrogance, had assumed that by marrying her he'd said all that needed to be said. And when her confidence in their relationship had faltered, it hadn't even occurred to him that he might bear some of the blame.

Swearing under his breath, he sprang from the bed and located her purse. Finding what he wanted, he curled it safely into his palm and prowled out onto the moonlit terrace but she wasn't there.

On the run again, he thought grimly.

Except this time he would track her down to the far corners of the earth if necessary.

In the end he didn't need to go as far as that. He found her in his study, curled up on one of the deep sofas with a book in her hands and Rambo and Terminator lying at her feet, her own personal guard. He remembered her poignant tale about the room she'd loved, with all the books. About pretending it was a library.

Thinking of the cold, loveless wasteland of her childhood years sickened him.

He understood now that reading had been her way of escaping from her world. And a way of making up for everything that was lacking in her life.

The dogs growled at his approach.

'It seems I have to fight my way through my own

dogs to talk to my wife.' He clicked his fingers and
Rambo immediately rose to his feet and moved but
Terminator stayed firmly by Laurel's side, his head
on his paws, refusing to leave her.

Cristiano had some sympathy for the dog because
he was feeling pretty much the same way.

He looked at the book in her hand, floored by
the enormity of what she'd achieved with her life.
'If you never had books as a child, how did you develop such an interest in reading?'

'I had a wonderful teacher at school. Miss Hayes.
She was very kind to me.' Laurel dropped her hand
onto the dog's head, her fingers caressing his smooth
fur. 'Don't send them away. I can't bear to be parted
from them after two years.'

Deciding that it was better to tolerate canine company than upset her further, Cristiano exchanged a
brief man to man warning glance with Terminator
just so that the dog knew who was in charge.

'Put the book down. I really need to talk to you.'

Slowly, she lowered the book to her lap but didn't
speak.

Cristiano wasn't finding it easy, either. 'I didn't
see our relationship the way you saw it. I can see
now that I took a great deal for granted.' Just when
it was imperative that the words spoken were perfectly matched to the situation, his habitual fluency
had deserted him. 'It's true that I may have been
guilty of a certain level of arrogance.'

Her gaze was steady. '*May* have been?'

'All right—I *was* arrogant, I admit it. I made far too many assumptions.' Trying to right a wrong, he paced from one side of the room to the other. 'But this whole situation has emerged because I didn't know what you were thinking. Yes, I was very much at fault, but you were also at fault in not telling me more about your past. Had you done so, I would have understood the reason you find it so hard to trust anyone and could have addressed it.'

'So then you would have added *reassure Laurel* to your bulging to-do list? I didn't want to be a project, Cristiano.'

'I didn't say that! *Maledezione*, give me a chance to explain myself!' His sudden explosion was greeted by a low warning growl from the dog by her side and Cristiano's mouth tightened. 'That animal is overprotective.'

'He loves me.'

'And apparently you accept that love without question whereas the rest of us have to work hard for that same degree of blind faith.' He ended that forceful declaration with a deep breath. 'I have never felt for any woman what I felt for you.'

'So you keep saying.'

'Speak again before I've finished and I'll find ways to silence you, dog or no dog,' he vowed, watching as her cheeks turned pink and she closed the book. 'I admit that I thought that by marrying you I'd demonstrated the depth of my feeling for you. I see now that I didn't spend enough time showing you how much I loved you but part of the reason for that was that I had no idea that you were having any doubts about my commitment to you. I made a terrible decision that day, but you have to believe that I didn't think you would lose the baby.'

Her cheeks turned a shade paler. 'Do we have to go over this again?'

'Yes, because we are not giving up on what we have so we have to both be clear about the way we feel. I married you because I loved you and wanted to spend the rest of my life with you. I didn't spend enough time making sure you knew that.' Acknowledging just how much damage that attitude had caused, he let out a long breath. 'You have to understand that that lapse on my part was to do with pressure of work, *not* because I felt less for you than I should have done. At worst I can be accused of complacency.'

'And arrogance.'

'Yes, we've already agreed that—' Cristiano spoke through his teeth '—but you didn't once come and tell me how you were feeling. I made mistakes, I admit it, but I made them because I believed everything to be good and strong with our marriage. You did *not* feel that way and yet you didn't tell me. Every time I gave you jewellery, you thanked me.

You suffered my mother's less than subtle comments without confiding in me.'

'She's your mother and you love her.'

And she'd never had that, he realised. She'd never had the luxury of knowing she was loved without question. Never been safely wrapped in the warmth of family. 'You are my wife and I love *you*. My first responsibility was to you. *Is* to you. Always.' He watched as her breathing turned shallow and discovered that he was holding his own breath as he waited for her response. 'Say something. But no more observations on my arrogance. That lesson is well and truly learned.'

'If we do this—' she left the word hanging vaguely '—what about the family you dreamed of having?'

'*You* are the family I dreamed of having and as for the rest—' ignoring the dogs, he leaned forward, removed the book from her hands and pulled her to her feet '—we'll find a way through it. But we'll find it together, not separately. Whatever you're thinking, you must share with me and this time I will be listening with both ears. *Ti amo*. I love you.' He scooped her face into his hands, feeling the softness of her skin against his palms. 'By the time I've finished proving it to you there will be no room for doubt in your head.'

There was a long silence and he discovered the true meaning of the word suspense.

He wondered what he was going to do if she backed off because he knew he was never going to accept no.

Those sea-green eyes held his. 'Hurt me again and there will be no second chances.'

'If I hurt you again, Terminator will eat me,' he drawled, opening a hand that wasn't quite steady to produce her wedding ring. 'This lives on your finger, not in your purse. Put it back on. And don't ever take it off again.'

CHAPTER NINE

'THIS is part of your plan to make me trust you? You're going to dangle me over the mouth of a volcano?' Laurel clutched the seat of the helicopter as she stared down at the lava fields and the mouth of the volcano with a mixture of fear and fascination. From here it was possible to see the main crater and she gave a shiver as she contemplated the raw, elemental power of nature and the potential for disaster.

Cristiano's pilot had flown the company helicopter from Palermo and picked them up for an aerial tour of this part of the island.

'Are we landing?'

'Not today. Today we are sightseeing in comfort.' His smile was so sinfully sexy that she couldn't look away from his mouth and that single glance was the catalyst for a blast of attraction so powerful that her head spun.

The days since they'd arrived had merged into one long, indulgent expression of their feeling for each other.

'Maybe that's enough sightseeing for one day,' she murmured, hating herself for being so weak. 'Shall we just go home?' Her heart increased its rhythm in the anticipation of what going home would mean. They were both insatiable, she thought. No matter how long they spent in bed they just couldn't get enough of each other. He was as hungry for her body as she was for his, which made his sudden tension all the more perplexing.

'We can't go home yet.'

'Why not?'

'Because I'm planning a surprise back at the house. I'm making a few changes.' More than that he wouldn't say and Laurel was intrigued. Over the days since he'd slid her wedding ring back onto her finger, they'd rarely spent any time in the house. He'd absented himself from her a few times to make some phone calls that she'd assumed had been business-related. Now she wasn't sure. What could he possibly be doing to an already perfect house that required her to be out of the way?

He already had a gym and a cinema room. What else was there in a house where life was mostly lived outdoors?

As the pilot took another sweep across the crater of the volcano she forgot about what was at home and instead just enjoyed being with Cristiano. He was a knowledgeable guide, his extensive knowledge of Etna derived from the geologists who worked with him as part of his company's expansion programme.

'We didn't do enough of this,' he said roughly when the helicopter finally landed back in the grounds of the house. 'We didn't spend enough time doing things together. Even when we were talking over dinner we were often discussing work.'

They strolled slowly back to the sun-baked terrace and Laurel accepted a glass of chilled Sicilian lemonade from one of the staff with a grateful smile.

'You don't have to apologise for being committed to your business. I'm as much of a workaholic as you are but yes, I agree that we failed to find a balance.' As a loud noise disturbed the peace, she turned her head towards the house. 'What's that banging?'

'It's part of your surprise.' He frowned impatiently and finished his drink. 'The noise is driving me mad. Let's go for a stroll.'

Laurel would have been quite happy to flop by the pool but caught the expression on his face and realised that he genuinely wanted to surprise her with whatever it was he was planning.

Intrigued as to what could possibly be happening in the house that required major refurbishment and secrecy, Laurel allowed him to propel her up the path that led through the citrus grove and together they walked towards the ruins of the Greco-Roman amphitheatre.

'Is your breathing all right?' He reached out and adjusted her hat to give her more protection from the fierce sun.

'Yes. Exercise isn't a trigger for me.' She paused to admire a tiny lizard, basking in the heat of the sun. 'Which is a relief or I'd have to give up my job.'

'Why did you choose fitness as a profession? Particularly with asthma.'

'The asthma was the reason.' The hot sun burned the back of her neck. 'I was determined to be as fit as possible. After that couple decided not to adopt me I tried ignoring the fact that I had asthma. I stopped using my inhaler, a decision that landed me in hospital a few times. After that I decided that it was more sensible to take a different approach so, instead of pretending I didn't have it, I tried to find out as much information as I could. One of the nurses in the hospital helped me. Everyone's asthma is different, of course, but for me exercise made a difference. The fitter I was, the healthier I was. For me the biggest trigger has always been stress.'

With a groan of remorse he pulled her against him. 'I feel like a brute for triggering that attack the night before Dani's wedding.'

It felt so good to be held. *To be loved.* 'If you hadn't, we might not have started talking again.'

'We would have done. There was no way I was ever letting you go again. From the moment you stepped onto the tarmac I was ready to lock you in my villa and never let you go. You felt it too.'

'Yes.' And the need to be with him had almost burned her alive. Even now she couldn't believe she was standing here with him. That, somehow, they'd reached this point.

She eased away from him and they walked among the ancient ruins hand in hand. 'I never grow tired of this place.' Oblivious to the other tourists, she sat down, admiring the amazing view of the sea with Mount Etna in the background. 'I wish we could live here.'

'You don't miss the city?'

'No. But living here isn't practical, is it?' Her tone regretful, she rubbed her fingers over the ancient stone and wondered about the generations of people who had sat in the same place before her. 'You can't run your business from here and neither can I. Maybe it isn't just the place. It's the fact that when we're here, we're not working.'

'So we both need to learn to compromise. We come here more often. Base ourselves here for, let's say, a week a month minimum?'

'That's a wonderful plan but in practice you'd be in your plane all the time, flying all over the world as usual.'

'Santo is taking over more of that side of the business.' Cristiano stretched out his long legs. 'He's the one scouting out potential sites for development and doing all the local negotiations with our lawyers. I've been spending more of my time here, overseeing things.'

Laurel laughed. 'The Emperor Cristiano, sitting on his throne?'

'That would be *King* Cristiano, surely, if I'm on a throne?' Smiling back at her, he curved his hand behind her neck and drew her face towards him for a kiss. 'Any time you want to prostrate yourself at my feet, just go right ahead.'

'In your dreams.' But even the mounting sizzle of sexual tension couldn't distract her from the conversation. Hope was a small tender bud, slowly unfurling inside her because finally this felt real. 'Do you think that could work, really? You could spend more time here in Taormina?'

'*We* could spend more time here. Although if we were commuting, I wouldn't drive. The helicopter is more practical.'

Laurel raised her eyebrows in disbelief. 'Have I ever pointed out how completely removed you are from real life? You say that as if it's a normal mode of transport.'

'It's a great option. With the helicopter, it doesn't really matter where I am. I can use that to fly around the island and also as a connection to the airport if I need the plane. And talking of planes—I have some good news. I didn't say anything before because I didn't want to raise your hopes.' He sounded supremely pleased with himself. 'I've tracked down a doctor who has agreed to talk to us about what happened before. He'll advise on whether there is anything that can be done. All we have to do is call him and tell him when it's convenient for us to see him.'

The warmth drained out of her. Suddenly she felt sick. 'I've already seen an expert. He told me I couldn't have children.'

'You saw a local doctor and let's face it, *angelo mia*, the local health care wasn't exactly impressive. You deserve better and I'm going to make sure you get it.'

Her heart was pounding. 'The team at the hospital saved my life.'

'True, but this is a specialist area. Huge advances have been made in recent years. I won't believe that there is no hope until I hear it from someone who knows what he's talking about. Don't argue. I want to do this for you. It's the least I can do.' His phone rang and she half expected him to ignore it as he had been doing but he took the call and immediately rose to his feet, otherwise he probably would have seen the change in her.

She sat, frozen.

The least he could do?

He had no idea.

And that was her fault, for not telling him how she felt.

Her hands started to shake and when he came off the phone, it was a struggle to behave normally. 'Who was that?'

'We need to get back to the house.'

Laurel was shaking so badly she wasn't sure her legs would hold her. 'I thought I was banned from seeing the house.'

'Not any more. I have a surprise for you. A gift.' As they negotiated the steps in the amphitheatre, he took her hand firmly in his and frowned. 'Your hands are cold. Are you all right?'

'I'm fine.'

She wanted to tell him that she didn't need big presents from him, that gifts weren't the reason she was with him but all she could think about was the fact that he was going to arrange for her to see a doctor and that was the last thing she wanted.

Cristiano lengthened his stride. 'I can't wait for you to see it.'

'The doctor?'

His glance was indulgent. 'I was talking about my gift to you.'

'Oh. I'm sure I'll love it,' she croaked, knowing that she had to tell him the truth.

They arrived back at the house and Cristiano immediately walked towards his study, one of her favourite rooms.

He paused with his hand on the door and she

wondered what on earth this gift was that merited so much drama in the presentation.

'You said I didn't think about what you really wanted. That the gifts I gave you weren't personal.' His voice was husky and he looked at her with expectant eyes. 'This gift is very personal and I hope it goes some way towards proving how much I love you.'

She wanted to tell him that it didn't matter how much he loved her, their relationship had no future if he was still hoping that there would be children, but there was no opportunity to speak because he was already pushing open the door and standing back, waiting for her reaction.

Laurel stared past him into the room and swallowed in disbelief.

What had once been a high-tech office—*his office*—had been transformed into a library. Tall bookshelves hand-carved in a beautiful pale wood lined the walls. Cristiano's desk had been removed and replaced with two large squashy sofas that just invited the visitor to sit down and relax and read. But what really drew her attention was the fact that the bookshelves were already stacked with books.

Laurel walked towards them on shaky legs, feeling a lump spring to the back of her throat. Running her eyes along the shelves, she saw old favourites as well as plenty she'd never read.

It should have been the perfect gift.

It would have been the perfect gift had it not been for the knowledge that their love had no future.

She remembered an occasion as a child when someone had given her a big shiny balloon, only for it to burst moments later.

Tilting her head back, she looked at the books. Her big shiny balloon. Reaching for one, she removed it from the shelf and glanced at the flyleaf. 'It's a first edition.'

'Yes. And before you say anything, I did have help tracking them down because I don't claim to be an expert on old books. But the idea was mine. And I gave them a list of the books. I made contact with that old English teacher you talked about, the estimable Miss Hayes, and she gave me some idea of what would be in a well stocked British library.'

The lump in her throat was big and solid and refused to budge. 'Miss Hayes? How did you find Miss Hayes?'

'I'm a man of influence, remember?' But his lazy drawl was tinged with something else. An uncertainty that she'd never heard in his tone before. 'Do you like it?'

'Oh, yes.' And the fact that he'd done this for her made everything else seem so much worse.

'I have something else for you.' He picked up a wrapped parcel from the table and handed it to her. 'I want you to read this book first.'

Laurel wondered why he'd chosen to wrap this

particular book. Removing the paper, she found herself holding a beautifully bound book of fairy tales.

'Oh—' Her voice cracked and she held it tightly, unable to speak as her emotions surged over her.

'You said you never had one as a child. I thought we should remedy that, but be warned—plenty of bad things happen in fairy tales.' Removing the book from her hands, he pulled her against him and lowered his mouth to hers. 'But just because bad things happen doesn't mean that you can't have a happy ending. Remember that. The Princess always gets the rich, handsome guy even if there are a few poisoned apples and spinning wheels along the way.'

Watching her happy ending retreating into the distance, Laurel swallowed.

He'd remembered her story about the bedroom full of books. About the fairy tales she'd never read.

'I don't know what to say.' Her voice cracked and he looked at her in consternation.

'I thought you'd be pleased. Happy.'

This was the moment she had to tell him she didn't want to see the doctor he'd found.

She *had* to explain.

'I am happy. And incredibly pleased. And so touched that you remembered—' The tears escaped and spilled over her cheeks and he gave a rough imprecation and crushed her against him.

'I realised that you were right when you said that

none of the presents I'd given you were personal. I made assumptions that a large diamond would be well received, never thinking that it wouldn't be special to you.'

'I feel really ungrateful now,' she muttered, clutching the book against her and pressing her damp face into his chest. 'It's not that I don't like diamonds. It's just that I know you've given away plenty and that they didn't signify love. But this—' she lifted her head and looked at the rows of books '—this is *so* special.'

'I would have built it myself for you but I wanted to spend the time with you and I wanted it to be a surprise. You missed out on a childhood. I wanted to give you an intensive course.' Carefully, he removed the book from her hands and set it down on the table.

Feeling utterly miserable, Laurel slid her arms around him. 'I love you.'

He gave a groan of relief and kissed her. 'Could you say that again?'

'I love you.' It was quite possibly the most honest moment of their marriage, the emotion as powerful an aphrodisiac as the physical attraction that consumed both of them.

Seconds later they were both naked on the rug, the shelves of books the only witness to their insatiable desire for each other.

One devastating kiss was all it took to turn her from a rational being to quivering, compliant, mindless, and the kiss didn't just involve their mouths, but their whole bodies, legs entwined, hands exploring. She dug her nails into his shoulders, feeling hard, sleek muscle and tensile strength. He slid his hand lower, his skilled fingers exploring her with unapologetic intimacy and his touch sent her from hot to scorching, every nerve-ending shimmering because he knew her body so well and he wasn't afraid to use that knowledge.

Her need for him was so acute that she moaned his name in a desperate plea and he shifted his position, clearly feeling the same urgency.

When he drove himself into her she cried out with relief because it felt so good. Her body immediately tightened around his and he swore softly in Italian, the dark glitter in his eyes revealing the effort required to hold back.

But she didn't want him to hold back and used everything she had to drive him wild, the gentle lick of her tongue and the sensuous slide of her hands teasing his heated flesh until he lost his grip on that legendary control of his and thrust deep into her body.

His mouth came down on hers in an intimate kiss and they were still kissing when they hit that inevitable peak. The explosion smashed through both of them, a sizzling, scorching shower of sexual ecstasy that left them both drained and exhausted.

* * *

Later, they swam in the pool, making the most of the shifting position of the setting sun. Light danced over the surface of the water, tiny flashes that sparkled and dazzled like the wink of a diamond.

It should have been perfect.

But Laurel was in agony.

'Cristiano—there's something I have to say to you—' The words burst from her and he took her in his arms, water clinging to his thick dark lashes.

'Then say it.'

'Earlier you said that you'd called an expert. I...I didn't realise that was what you wanted. When you said that being married to me was more important to you than having children, I didn't realise that you were planning on seeing doctors and doing everything we could to have a baby.'

'I wanted to do that for you.'

'Did you? Or did you want to do it for yourself?'

His eyes narrowed. 'You don't want me to do that?'

She could have lied. She could have let the relationship drift on without telling him the truth but they'd stumbled over enough obstacles in their marriage without her laying new ones.

'No.' She shook her head slowly, knowing that what she was about to say could kill their future. 'No, I don't. There's something I haven't told you. Something I haven't been quite honest about.'

He was still, his face shadowed by the rapidly diminishing light. 'Go on.'

How did she explain? Where did she begin? 'Losing our baby was the worst thing that had ever happened to me. When I felt those first pains I thought to myself, *No, please no, anything but this.* I was frantic. There was nothing, *nothing*, I wanted in the world as much as our child.' Her eyes filled as she remembered the horror of those few days. 'And I lost it. And when they told me I couldn't have more children I didn't even care because I didn't want to *think* about more children. All I cared about was the baby I'd lost. There was no way, *no way*, I ever would have put myself through that again. Risked that again. Our marriage was wrecked anyway so the issue of not being able to have more children became irrelevant.'

He inhaled deeply. 'Do you still feel that way?'

'Yes.' She wasn't going to lie to him. 'Even if it *were* possible, which it isn't, I wouldn't put myself through that again. For me, being pregnant wasn't about excitement and expectation, it was about fear and terrible loss.'

'Laurel—' A muscle flickered in his jaw and she saw the guilt in his eyes but she also knew that guilt was misplaced.

'This isn't about what happened between us, Cristiano. Even if you *had* been here, it wouldn't have changed the outcome for that pregnancy. At the time you accused me of overreacting and in a way you were right—' For the first time ever, she realised that it was true. 'I was devastated and the way I coped with that was to push you away. If I'd just yelled at you there would have come a point where you wanted me to talk about what happened and I just couldn't. All I wanted to do was hide.'

'So you left.'

'I was so wrong to do that.' The tears spilled from her eyes. 'I was grieving and heartbroken and I took it out on you. I blamed you for everything. And I just couldn't tell you how I was feeling.'

'But now you have—' His own voice decidedly unsteady, he pulled her hard against him, crushing her against him. 'And now I understand what you want, there will be no more talk of experts.'

Her face was buried in his neck, her tears mingling with the water from the pool. 'What about what *you* want?'

'I want you.' His tone was unmistakably possessive and he eased her away from him so that he could look at her. 'You. Always. I thought I'd made that clear.'

'If you'd married a different woman you could have had a different life.'

He leaned his forehead against hers. 'I wouldn't want any life that didn't have you in it.'

She felt light inside, and strangely relaxed. It was as if sharing the heaviest of her thoughts had somehow reduced their weight. And his unquestioning acceptance of the way things were gave her courage. 'There's something else—something I've been thinking about for a while but never mentioned to anyone. I don't know how you're going to feel about it.'

'Try me and let's find out.'

Laurel hesitated because she truly had no idea how he was going to react to what she was going to say. 'What I'd really love is for us to adopt a child.' The words rushed out of her. 'And not just because there's no chance of having our own. I want us to give a child a home. Not a baby—everyone wants to adopt babies. I mean an older child. A lost, lonely child who has no idea how it feels to be wanted. I want to do up a bedroom and fill it with toys and books but most of all I want to be a loving family to someone who doesn't have that and has no hope of that.'

'Yes, I want that too.' It was characteristic of his generosity that he didn't hesitate. 'Hearing what you went through horrifies me. And we have so much. I would very much like to give a secure home and family to a child in need of one. I've been thinking the same thing myself since you told me about your experience. And you would be an amazing mother.'

His positive response moved her more than anything else he'd said to her or done for her.

Her heart opened to him and she slid her arms

around him, feeling the hardness of male muscle under her seeking fingers. 'You're very special.'

One eyebrow lifted. 'I thought I was an arrogant, controlling workaholic?'

'That too.' But she knew that this needed so much more to make it work than just words and good intentions. 'Are you sure? I don't suppose it's going to be easy.'

He gave a wicked smile and gently lowered his mouth to hers. 'You know I love a challenge.'

They stayed in the *castello*, time drifting, until their idyll was fractured by a phone call from Santo.

Cristiano's heart sank as he listened as his brother outlined the work crisis that couldn't be solved without his attention.

His gaze flickered to Laurel, still sleeping in the bed, her naked limbs and the curve of her hip creating a visual feast.

The temptation to live out the rest of their days in this paradise was powerful. Here, it was impossible for her to hide from him. Cocooned in their own private world, they'd been protected from reality. He wasn't fool enough to think that this idyll could continue back in the real world. He had a business to run and so did she. The pressures on him were enormous and no matter how much effort he put into juggling his priorities, there were going to be times when they would be parted.

Reluctant to wake her, he pulled on his clothes and took the phone and his conversation out onto the terrace. He made himself a *caffé*, the small dense espresso that he favoured at the start of the day, and listened to his brother whilst at the same time thinking about the challenges facing his marriage.

He knew they'd come a long way in the past few weeks. What he didn't know was whether it was far enough—whether what they'd created could survive when they returned to the outside world and he was no longer able to devote all his attention to the relationship.

Their marriage was like a boat, he thought, watching as a yacht skimmed the sparkling water of the Bay of Naxos. He'd shored up the hull and made the necessary repairs. Here in port, what they had looked strong and seaworthy. Whether it was strong enough to survive in open water he didn't know. And there was only one way to find out.

Having listened to Santo, he delivered the necessary advice and instruction and then ended the call and finished his coffee.

Beneath him the surface of the pool reflected the perfect blue sky and behind him the early morning sun shone on Etna's summit.

'Is everything OK?' Her voice came from behind him and he turned to see her sitting up in the bed, her eyes sleepy and her mouth temptingly rosy.

Without make-up, her hair tangled from too much midnight loving, she was gorgeous.

His woman.

'Everything is fine.' He found himself postponing the moment he had to break the news that they were leaving but she obviously sensed something and slid out of bed, deliciously unselfconscious.

Neither hiding nor flaunting, she reached for the wisp of cream silk that had started the night on her body and ended it in a discarded pool on the bedroom floor. That simple movement was all it took to have him forgetting his coffee and when she joined him on the terrace he slid his hand behind her neck and drew her in for a long, slow kiss.

'Mmm—' reluctantly she pulled away '—what is it you're not telling me?'

'What makes you so sure there's something I'm not telling you?'

'The look on your face.' Her arms slid around his neck. 'Tell me.'

There was no easy way to break news he knew she didn't want to hear. 'I need to go back for a while. A crisis is brewing with the Sardinia development that needs my attention. *Mi dispiace, angelo mia.* I'm sorry.'

He expected disappointment but instead she smiled. 'It's fine. We knew we couldn't stay here for ever.' It was a brave statement that concealed her disappointment and Cristiano swore under his breath.

'*Don't* tell me it's fine while all the time thinking something different. Tell me what you're thinking. I want to know.'

'All right.' She sat back on her heels, a gleam of humour lighting her eyes. 'I'm thinking I don't want you to go. I want us to stay here for ever.'

He breathed a sigh of relief. 'At least now I know you're being honest.'

'But we both know it isn't practical to stay here. And this deal is really important to you, I understand that. I know how long you waited for this one. You can't delegate it to anyone else.'

He took her face in his hands and kissed her hard. 'Whatever the world throws at us, it doesn't change how much I love you. Tell me you understand that.'

'Yes.'

Over the past few days she'd opened up more than she had at any time in their marriage but he was under no illusions. When Laurel felt threatened, she closed the world out. That was the way she protected herself. Here, he'd refused to let her hide but he was realistic enough to know that once they were back in the busy world they inhabited, things would change.

'One week,' he promised against her lips, 'we'll go back for one week. And we will be together at the beginning and end of every day. Breakfast every morning and dinner every evening. Sardinia is only a short hop away from Sicily. I won't be gone long. That's a promise.'

CHAPTER TEN

LAUREL watched as Cristiano sent an email with one hand while tying the knot of his silk tie with the other. A cup of cold coffee lay untouched on the table because he hadn't had a moment to drink it. From the moment they'd arrived back at the Palazzo Ferrara, the Palermo home that had been in his family for generations, he'd been swamped with work.

She felt a sharp pang of longing for the simplicity of their life in Taormina, missing the closeness and the lack of outside intrusion. Now she had to share him with a million other people. Yes, he'd kept to his promise of sharing breakfast and dinner with her but last night's dinner hadn't been served until gone eleven o'clock.

And the grandeur of the Palazzo unsettled her.

Her eyes roved over the priceless art on the walls. Cristiano was a renowned collector and she knew he was responsible for much of the restoration of the Palazzo. But although he spent time here when he needed to be in the city, she knew his preference would always be the villa at the Ferrara Spa and their new home in Taormina.

Their home.

Thinking of somewhere as home sent a warm feeling flowing through her. Watching as he took a phone call, switching easily between English and Italian, she felt her insides soften because this incredible man was *hers*. Yes, he was a workaholic but she loved his energy and his utter commitment to a task. And to his family. Cristiano was big on responsibility and commitment and those had been rare qualities in her life before she'd met him. He was offering her that part of himself.

Laurel took over tying his tie, ducking as he gesticulated with his hands and let out a stream of angry Italian to the person on the end of the phone.

When he finally cut the connection he was visibly angry.

'Lawyers!' His jaw clenched, he stood still while she straightened his tie. 'They are enough to drive a man to drink. I have to fly to Sardinia and I'd planned to spend the afternoon with you. I was going to take you shopping and spoil you.'

'I'll be fine. Dani is back from her honeymoon and we're meeting at the Spa later for manicures and a girly chat. I also promised Santo I'd take a look at the health club at the Resort. I'm going to do a workout, observe some of the trainers in action. Make some recommendations. Then I'm going to find myself an empty office and answer all those emails I've been ignoring since we went to Taormina.'

Cristiano frowned. 'You can use my office, but I don't want you to have to work today.'

'I don't have to work. I want to work.' Laurel stood back, wondering if there was ever going to be a time when she didn't go weak at the knees when she looked at him. 'There. You look smart.'

Sinfully handsome, she thought.

Hers.

'Grazie.' Distracted, Cristiano reached for his jacket. 'I will be back in time to take you for dinner tonight and that's a promise. I've discovered a new restaurant—'

'In that case I'll buy a new dress.'

'You do that.' He leaned forward and kissed her. 'I have spoken to my mother, by the way. She was mortified that you'd been through that without telling anyone. She wished very much that you had confided in her.'

Laurel shrugged awkwardly. 'Not my forte, as you know.'

'I tried to explain to her but I didn't want to talk about your past without your permission.' He rubbed the backs of his fingers over her cheek. 'You *could* confide in her. It would help her understand.'

'She just wants you to be happy. I do understand that.'

He pulled her hard against him and wrapped his

arms around her. 'I *am* happy. How could I not be happy when I have you?'

His phone buzzed again and he gave an exasperated sigh and released her. 'I miss Taormina,' he said regretfully and she wanted to tell him that she did too but he was already walking out of the door and she knew that by the time he was in the car he would have forgotten her because no one had more focus than Cristiano.

At the moment all his attention was on sorting out the deal in Sardinia.

The most important deal to him for a long time.

'I'm so clever.' Delighted with herself, Dani waggled pink toenails and adjusted the brim of her hat. 'I knew that if I got you together you wouldn't be able to keep your hands off each other. You just can't help yourselves. And now Cristiano is close to closing the Sardinia deal so it's happy ever afters all round.'

Laurel sat cross-legged on the sun lounger next to her. 'What is so important about Sardinia?'

'It was our father's dream.' Dani rubbed more suncream into her legs. 'He wanted hotels on both islands. But it's tricky buying land for development there. Cristiano found the perfect spot, of course, because he's a genius. And then he has this way of making people feel as if they can't not sell to him. That's why he has to be there to finalise the deal.

He's the one they're selling it to. They trust him to do the right thing. To develop the land in a sympathetic way that won't ruin the environment. How was Taormina?'

'Beautiful.'

'It's such a romantic place.' Dani admired her pink toenails. 'It must have been like a second honeymoon for you. Any time you want to thank me for getting you two back together, just go right ahead.'

Laurel laughed. 'You don't give up, do you?'

'No. And now I'm moving straight on to Plan B.'

'Cristiano and I are back together.' Laurel shifted into a more comfortable position. 'We don't need Plan B.'

'Ah—Plan B isn't getting back together. Plan B is about having babies.' Dani had her face turned towards the sun, otherwise she would have seen Laurel tense. 'Don't you think it would be fun to be pregnant at the same time? Our children could play together. Grow up together like I did with my cousins.'

She couldn't accuse her friend of insensitivity, Laurel thought numbly, because she'd never told her the details of what had happened. But she had to. This was the time.

'Dani—'

'It's no good. I can't keep a secret.' Dani sat up and pushed her hat away from her face. Her eyes shone. 'I'm pregnant. I did the test last night.

Raimondo wants me to wait a few weeks to tell everyone but you're not everyone.'

Laurel was stunned. 'You were pregnant when you got married?'

'No, I was not!' Dani's voice was an outraged squeak. 'And keep your voice down. Do you think I want my brothers to beat Raimondo to a pulp? This is a honeymoon baby.' She looked content and pleased with herself.

'But you've only been married for two weeks.'

'Three.' Dani laughed. 'You obviously weren't wasting time looking at your watch when you were in Taormina. I've been married for three whole weeks.'

Laurel stared at her. *Three* weeks?

But—dear God, Dani was right. It had been three weeks. Which meant that—

She felt the blood drain from her face and dimly saw Dani's concerned frown.

'Laurie? Are you OK?'

'It's the heat,' Laurel muttered. 'I might go and lie down for a while. I don't feel well.'

'What do you mean, you don't feel well?' Dani's face lit up. 'Maybe you're pregnant too. Oh, my God, that would be awesome.'

'No! I mean—that isn't possible.'

'Why not? You've been having sex non-stop for the past three weeks. Here—' Dani dug around in her bag and pressed a slim packet into Laurel's hand. 'I bought two and I don't need this one. You take it.'

It was a pregnancy test.

Laurel's mouth was dry.

Why would a woman who couldn't possibly get pregnant need to take a pregnancy test?

'I don't need this. I can't be pregnant.'

'That's what I thought,' Dani said happily. 'Turned out I was wrong. Look, do you want to—'

'I have to go and lie down.' Her head spinning, Laurel walked away from her friend, bumped into a chair and stumbled down the steps to the beach.

She couldn't be pregnant.

Ten minutes later she was sitting in the empty villa, staring at a positive pregnancy test and swallowing down the bitter taste of fear.

It was happening all over again, except this time she'd skipped the moments of anticipatory joy and jumped straight into deep, dark terror.

Hand shaking, she rummaged in her bag for her phone and punched in his number.

When it went straight to voicemail she felt a rush of panic because she'd so badly wanted him to answer. 'Cristiano?' She tried hard to keep her voice steady but somehow it came out as a desperate whisper. *Oh, God, she was going to sound needy and pathetic.* And then she remembered that his phone was off because he was finalising the Sardinian deal. How could she have forgotten that? He didn't have time to nursemaid her. It wasn't fair of her to put him in this position. The urge to beg him to come home was almost desperate but she tightened her grip on the phone and forced the words through the panic. 'I just called to wish you luck in your meeting.'

Cristiano was about to go into the most important meeting of his life when his phone rang.

It was Santo, calling with a final set of figures for him.

Armed with everything he needed to close the deal, Cristiano ended the call and then noticed that he had a message waiting.

'Cristiano?' Carlo looked at him expectantly and Cristiano nodded, checking his voicemail as he walked through to the meeting room.

He stopped dead as he heard Laurel's voice.

'Cristiano? I just called to wish you luck in your meeting.'

She must have called in those same few minutes he'd been talking to Santo.

He frowned, oblivious to the men around the table, all waiting for him to start the meeting. Why would she be calling to wish him luck?

He'd seen her that morning and she'd wished him luck in person.

'Cristiano?' Carlo's voice was more urgent this time but Cristiano lifted a hand to silence him.

'I need to make a call. Excuse me.' Leaving Carlo to keep the conversation going, Cristiano stepped out of the room and dialled Laurel's number but there was no reply.

Cursing under his breath, he checked his watch. She was supposed to be sitting by the pool gossiping with his sister.

Frowning, he played the message again and this time he heard the change in her tone. *The long pause between saying his name and wishing him luck.*

He played it again.

'Cristiano?'

Something was wrong.

He called his sister but, predictably, her phone was engaged.

'Cristiano?' Carlo was standing in the doorway. 'What the hell is going on? They're waiting for you. It's taken five years to get to this point.'

Cristiano tried Laurel's number one more time but her phone was switched off.

Laurel never phoned him when he was working. She'd only ever done it once before.

Following an instinct that he couldn't even identify, Cristiano was already on his way out of the door. 'You'll have to handle this without me.'

His lawyer looked stunned. 'But—'

It was too late.

Cristiano was gone.

* * *

Laurel was sitting in a shivering heap on the floor of the luxurious bathroom when the door to the villa crashed open and she heard Cristiano thundering her name.

Purposeful footsteps echoed in the distance and then the bathroom door flew open.

He swore when he saw her. 'What's happened? What are you doing in here?'

Her teeth were chattering and she felt pathetically relieved to see him. 'You came.'

'Of course I came, although next time I'd rather you avoided the cryptic and went straight for the direct approach. Your message was total nonsense.' Brows locked together in a concerned frown, he scooped her off the floor and carried her through to the bedroom. She expected him to deposit her on the bed but he didn't. Instead he sat down, holding her securely on his lap. 'Now tell me what's wrong, *tesoro*. Is it your asthma?'

'No.' She couldn't stop shivering but instantly she felt better inside just because he was there.

'Laurel?' He held her firmly while he waited for her to talk, but talking wasn't easy.

Her teeth chattered. Her insides churned. She felt horribly sick. Sick?

Oh, God.

'I'm pregnant.'

He turned to stone. 'I thought you told me—'

'I told you what they told me. That I couldn't get

pregnant. They said it wasn't possible.' Her voice rose and he spoke to her softly in Italian, his own fears carefully hidden as he tried to calm her.

'Laurel, I know you're afraid but it's going to be all right. You have to trust me. This is *good* news, *angelo mia.*'

'No.' Her eyes pooled with tears. 'I can't have a baby, Cristiano. Just because I'm pregnant doesn't mean I'm capable of having this baby. Last time—'

'This time will be different.' He said that with an absolute certainty that at any other time would have driven her to tease him for his arrogance but right now she was past teasing.

'You don't know that.'

'And you don't know that it won't be.' He smoothed her hair with hands that were strong and capable.

'The doctors told me I couldn't get pregnant. They said it wasn't possible or I would have made you use contraception.'

'So I don't think those will be the doctors whose advice we are seeking now.' He didn't release his hold on her as he pulled his phone out of his pocket.

Her breath juddered. 'You need a new phone.'

'I am quite attached to this one. The crack in it reminds me of what is important in life.' He dialled a number, spoke in rapid Italian and then ended the call. 'I already told you I had done some research. This doctor I have found has extensive experience of your condition. I am arranging an appointment immediately.'

'What if he can't fit me in?'

'It's a she,' Cristiano said mildly, 'and if she can't come to us then we will go to her.'

For the first time since she'd discovered she was pregnant, Laurel felt herself relax slightly. 'You were in the middle of a meeting. I can't believe you came.'

'Did you really think I wouldn't?'

'Today was so important to you.' She felt a rush of guilt. 'I've ruined everything.'

'No, you haven't. But I'm confused as to why you didn't just ask me to come in your message? You said my name in such a desperate voice and then wished me luck. I was left playing guessing games.'

'I'd forgotten about your meeting. When the test result was positive I panicked and phoned you. I was so desperate to speak to you and then when the phone went through to voicemail I remembered where you were and what you were doing and that of *course* you would have switched your phone off.'

'I didn't switch my phone off. I must have been on the phone to Santo when you called.'

'I hadn't thought of that. I realised I was being unfair to you so I just muttered something stupid about good luck.'

'I listened to the message again and I heard the difference in your voice between the moment you started to speak and the end.' He breathed deeply. 'I'm so pleased you called me.'

'You're pleased I've blown the most important deal of your career?'

'That isn't important. What is important is that you were in trouble and you turned to me. And not only that, you did it without thinking. That's good news. And now for our other piece of good news—' he placed his hand on her stomach and gave a slow masculine smile. 'Did I or did I not warn you that I would make you pregnant again? I am super-virile, no?'

Her face was still damp with tears but a tiny smile broke free. 'Super-arrogant.'

'I am simply looking at the facts. I *have* made you pregnant.'

Laurel sniffed and punched him lightly on the shoulder, laughing as he'd intended. 'I suppose you think I'm a lucky woman.'

'That goes without saying.' His grip on her tightened and his voice was husky. 'And I am a lucky man because you gave me the greatest gift you could give anyone. You turned to me. You trusted me.'

'And you came.'

'I will always come. I will always be here for you and for our family. From now on I am dedicating my life to standing between you and stress. You won't need that inhaler because you have me.'

Her eyes stung again. 'Overprotective.'

'Sicilian.' Unapologetic, he kissed her gently. 'And completely crazy about you.'

EPILOGUE

THE terrace was filling up with people and Laurel watched from the master bedroom as a steady stream of expensive cars came down the long drive that led to the *castello*. The dips and potholes had long since been smoothed away, the wildness of the almond orchards tamed in readiness for this celebration.

Virtually the only thing that was in its original form was the old rusty key he'd given her.

She kept that in a drawer by her bed.

'What are you doing in here?' Cristiano's deep voice came from behind her. 'They're waiting for you on the terrace.'

'I came up to find Elena's stuffed bunny and then she fell asleep on the bed. The excitement has worn her out.' Her expression softening, Laurel turned to check on their little daughter, now splayed like a starfish in the centre of their huge bed in the pale yellow dress that Cristiano's mother had given to her as a gift. At the foot of the bed the two dogs lay guarding their little charge, refusing to budge. 'I'm trying to keep her clean for the party.'

'An uphill battle, I should think,' Cristiano drawled, well aware of his daughter's adventurous nature. 'Dani and Raimondo have arrived with Rosa. She's desperate to see her cousin. All she can say is "Lena".'

'Elena is excited about seeing her, too. They're the best of friends.'

'And talking of friends—' Dani virtually danced into the room, looking delighted with herself as she hugged Laurel. 'I predict they're going to be celebrating their birthday together for the rest of their lives. Another one of my perfect plans. Why are you all hiding up here? You should be downstairs greeting your guests.'

'I've delegated that task to Santo—' Cristiano kissed his sister and then stooped and retrieved the stuffed toy from under the bed. 'Is this what you were looking for?'

Woken by the sound of her father's voice, Elena opened her eyes sleepily and Laurel felt her insides melt with love as she watched him scoop the child into his arms along with the bunny.

'Rosa?' Yawning widely, Elena looked round the room hopefully and Laurel smiled.

'Come on then. Let's go and find your cousin and get this party started.'

'Oh, please let me take her—' Dani stretched out

her arms and prised her niece away from Cristiano. 'We'll see you downstairs when you're ready, won't we Elena? Your cousin Rosa has already found the chocolate fountain so I hope your *mamma* doesn't expect this dress to stay pale yellow for long.'

Laughing, Laurel kissed her daughter's smooth cheek. 'Happy Birthday, sweetheart. Go with your aunt. We'll be there in a minute.'

Elena's cheeks dimpled and then she was wriggling out of Dani's arms and running out of the door in search of her cousin with her aunt and the dogs in hot pursuit.

'Can you believe she's only two? She's so confident and happy.' Laurel watched her go, knowing that the reason her daughter was so secure was that she'd always been surrounded by close family and Cristiano confirmed that with his next words.

'She's confident because she knows how much she is loved.'

Laurel turned and saw the file in Cristiano's hand. 'What's that?'

Slowly, he put it down on the bed and took her hands. 'It's what we've been waiting for.'

Her heart skipped. Nerves danced in her stomach. 'Really? It's actually going to happen? I didn't allow myself to think it. I didn't even dare ask about progress in case I jinxed it.'

'Everything is signed and approved. It's done.'

It had taken two years, unbelievable amounts of

red tape not to mention Cristiano's power and influence, but they'd persisted and it seemed that finally that persistence was to be rewarded.

Somewhere in a children's home in Italy, a lonely girl called Chiara was spending her last night with no family.

Laurel felt her eyes fill. 'When can we fetch her?'

'Tomorrow.' Frowning slightly, he lifted his hand and gently brushed away her tears. 'You know this isn't going to be easy, don't you? I'm worried you're expecting it to be smooth and I'm expecting significant bumps, at least at the beginning.'

'I *know* it won't be smooth. Life isn't smooth, but it's the bumps that help us find out who we are. And it's handling the bumps that gives us courage.' She looked up at him, marvelling at how much she'd changed in just a few years. *Because of him*, she thought. He made her feel safe. And the knowledge that she was truly loved gave her the courage to express herself freely. 'For a while I was worried that because we'd managed to have Elena, you wouldn't want to go through with this.'

'Not once did that thought cross my mind.'

Moved, she leaned her head against his chest. 'Do you ever wish we could have had more children of our own?'

'Honestly? No. I couldn't put you through that again and frankly I couldn't put myself through it, either. The worry almost killed me. I'm just relieved that you and Elena are safe,' he groaned, pulling her against him and hugging her tightly. 'We have a beautiful, healthy daughter and each other, and another daughter on the way. I always quit when I'm on a winning streak.'

Laurel heard the sounds of happy, excited children playing and tilted her head. 'Listen.' Above the shrieks and giggles, Elena's little voice floated across to them. 'Do you know what that is?'

'What?'

Laurel smiled happily and took his hand. 'I could be wrong, but I think it's the sound of a happy ending.'

'Either that or it's a bunch of children about to destroy the tranquillity of our infinity pool.' But his hand tightened on hers as they walked towards the terrace to greet their family.

* * * * *